Also by Rosemary Edghill

SPEAK DAGGERS TO HER

A Bast Mystery

Rosemary Edghill

TOR ®

A TOM DOHERTY ASSOCIATES BOOK
NEW YORK

SPEAK DAGGERS TO HER

Cover art by Dierdre E. Snowdon

A Tor Book
Published by Tom Doherty Associates, Inc.
175 Fifth Avenue
New York, NY 10010

Tor Books on the World-Wide Web:
http://www.tor.com

Tor® is a registered trademark of Tom Doherty Associates, Inc.

ISBN: 0-812-53438-7
Library of Congress Catalog Card Number: 94-116

First edition: May 1994
First mass market edition: December 1995

Printed in the United States of America

0 9 8 7 6 5 4 3 2 1

I will speak daggers to her, but use none.

—Shakespeare *(Hamlet)*

I

I could say this was any large Eastern city, but you'd know it was New York. I could say my name was Isobel Gowdie, or Janet Kyteler, or even Tam Lin, but what's on my paychecks and phone bills isn't important. My name—my real name—is Bast.

I live in New York and I'm a Witch.

Put away your pitchforks—or more likely, here in the nineties, stifle your yawns and stop edging toward the door. It's just my religion, into which I put about as much time and money as you do into whatever you do that isn't for the biweekly paycheck. I'm not inclined to criticize any way a person might have found to waste excess money, and I'm not having as much fun as you probably imagine I'm having. No naked orgies under the moon, for example; the Parks Commission would object and it's no way to have safe sex. When modern Witches meet, the main concern is usually how to fit eight people and the couch into a room the size of a Manhattan living room *and* make sure you leave with your own Reeboks. No lubricious fantasy there.

Just one more thing about the W word and then I'll leave it, since it's a subject that either bores you silly or you've got all the wrong ideas and won't change them for anything I say. Personally, I'd rather we called ourselves anything else, from Pagans to Earth Religionists to Aquarians. It would fit most of us better: over-educated ex-hippies trying to unscrew the inscrutable, trying to make sense of life through ritual and gnosis. But we got stuck with the W word back in the forties, when a lovely half-mad Brit picked up Dr. Margaret Murray's anthropological dream-mongering about the witch trials in western Europe and tried to weave a modern religion out of it, patching and piecing from everything that caught his fancy.

By the time Gerald B. Gardner was done, his *"wicca-craften"* had damn little resemblance to the Witches out of history and fairy tales, and so do we. Now we're stuck with the name and a tag-end of faded glory that some of us spend a lot of time justifying to anyone who shows the least interest.

I don't. What I was trying to justify, this particular Friday, was a left-hand margin the typesetter had accidentally set ragged and the client didn't want to pay to get reset. Since the typesetter didn't want to eat the cost and reset it for free, that left me, a Number 10 single-sided razor blade, and a lot of freelance hours.

The Bookie Joint—Houston Graphics if I answer the phone before 5:00—is one of those places you've never heard of unless you're in the business—a freelance studio that does layout and pasteup, turning piles of typeset galleys into pages of type. They call the people who do it art- ists, which is the only glamorous thing about the job. Layout artist is a dead-end job in a dying field; most books these days are set page-for- page, and desktop publishing is taking over for the really small presses.

But if you don't mind earning less than ten dollars an hour with no bennies and no guaran- tees, it's a great job. Everybody who works here is something else—actors, writers, artists. Your schedule is flexible to fit around your other jobs. You can get as many or as few hours a week as you need—except when something like the job in front of me comes up. I'd promised Raymond I'd finish it before I left tonight. He's our art di- rector and takes it almost as seriously as he does modern dance. Ray's a dancer—at least he was while he still had his knees. We have some framed stills on the walls. Jazz Ballet of Harlem. Pretty.

Ragged left instead of ragged right. You'd think StereoType never typeset a sheaf of poems before.

The phone rang and I was glad to answer it.

"Bookie-Joint-Can-I-Help-You?"

"Bast?"

This narrowed the caller down to a member of my immediate world.

"Bast?"

"Yo?"

"Miriam's dead."

It was Lace on the phone, which meant that Miriam was Miriam Seabrook, and Miriam was my age. People in their middle thirties don't just up and die.

"Bast?" Lace sounded half a step away from hysteria. "We were going out to dinner and I used my key and she was lying there on the bed and I thought she was asleep—" Lace took a deep breath and started to cry in high, weepy yelps.

"Did you call the police?"

I thought I was fine—after all, I wasn't the one who'd walked in and found my lover dead—but my jaw muscles ached when I pushed the words out. Not Miriam. Not dead. I didn't even know her very well, I plea-bargained.

"I can't. You know I can't. You know what they'll do to me—oh, please, *please*, can't you come over?" Lace started to cry in earnest, a real Irish peening for the healins.

Lace is a dyke radical, which means she has a lot of not-quite-paranoid fantasies about what the Real World will do to her just for breathing. Not quite paranoid, because her mother got a custody order to take her kids away from her and the U.S. government revoked her passport when she came out of the closet. She used to be some kind of engineer until she joined the lunatic fringe.

"Lace. Listen. Call 911 and tell them. You don't have to tell them who you are. Just do it. I'll be right over."

Muffled breathing. Too late *i* wondered if Miriam had been murdered and was the murderer still lurking around her apartment waiting to make it two for two.

"Lace? Are you there?" Fear is contagious; I was all alone in the studio and it had seemed a friendly place until the phone rang. I could see late afternoon sunbeams white with dust. Sunshine. Daytime. Normalcy. Right?

"Lace."

"I'm here." A tiny little whisper.

"I'll be there as soon as I can, okay? Okay?"

Lace hung up on me.

I barely remembered to lock all three of the inside locks at Houston Graphics, and I was halfway down the block before I realized I'd forgotten to lock the inside lobby door. By then I had no intention of going back.

New Yorkers are supposed to have this inborn instinct for getting cabs. I don't. Hell, I can't even figure out the bus routes. Fortunately, Miriam's is right on the subway. I caught the D at Broadway/Lafayette, changed to the A at 59th Street, and headed uptown.

I got off at the 211th Street stop, staggered up the stairs (still under construction, as they have been for ever and aye) to the late afternoon howl of sirens and car horns, and into the building on Park Terrace East.

No answer on the buzzer. I punched buttons at random until somebody who should have known better buzzed me in. The elevator was broken so I took the stairs, and by now I was sure what I was going to find.

Fifth floor. Five flights up. Miriam's door was open.

My mouth tasted like burnt copper. I almost called for Miriam, but Miriam was dead, so I heard, unless it had all been somebody's idea of a sick joke.

"Lace?"

I stood in the open doorway. The apartment sounded empty. So I went in and hunted through the whole place real fast. No alien muggers with chain saws. No Lace, either, and no way of knowing whether she'd called the cops. Her set of keys to Miriam's place was on the living room table, right where she'd probably dropped them.

Miriam was in the bedroom on the bed. And she was dead.

I don't know why they always say in books that people weren't sure or couldn't quite believe it. You *know*—in the pit of your stomach, instantly, beyond doubt. This is no longer a person.

She didn't look quite real—like a waxworks, almost-not-quite life-size. She had on her underpants and a khaki T-shirt, and she was flopped there just like she'd gone to sleep. There was a wet spot on the sheet—gritty reality of the relaxed sphincter—but the sense of peace, and rest, and *absence* was almost numbing.

Or maybe I was just in shock.

For something to do I went back out and put Lace's keys in my purse. It'd been over an hour since she'd called me, and it was starting to look like a safe bet Lace hadn't phoned 911. I wondered why she'd phoned me.

So I could do it, of course. And I knew I was going to, which irritated me. But first I was going to take another look around the place, which wasn't as stupid at a time like this as it sounds. Miriam was a wannabe Witch, and a Neopagan, and I didn't want a bunch of people who couldn't tell the difference between that and Anton LaVey splashing "Satanist" all over the *New York Post*.

But all the posters on the walls looked more feminist than anything else, and no one who didn't know what they were looking at would recognize Miriam's altar.

I went back to Miriam. Priestess of the Goddess and death is all part of the Great Cycle of Rebirth and all that crap, but I still didn't want to touch her. She had an intense perfume, like a cross between pine needles and fresh bread. I couldn't concentrate on anything, and all the details except the body on the bed kept slipping away. Finally I made myself hook my fingernail under the silver box-chain around Miriam's neck. It would be just as well if she didn't go to the morgue wearing a pentacle.

Morgue. Miriam was dead. Damn it, she was *my* age, maybe even a few years younger, and people my age just don't curl up and die.

And now I was stripping the body so no one would know she was a Neopagan.

And I call *Lace* the paranoid one.

I was more keyed up than I thought, which was why I yelped and jumped and jerked the chain so her head rolled toward me as the pendant slipped out of her shirt.

Because Miriam wasn't wearing a pentacle—that nice chaste star-in-a-circle that's the badge of office of practically everyone here on the New Aquarian Frontier. What Miriam was wearing on that long silver chain was little and brown and nasty, and eventually my heart slowed down and I saw it was a mummified bird claw of some kind, with the stump wrapped in silver wire so she could string it on the chain. The nails were painted red.

"Oh, *fuck . . .*" I said very softly. Then I unhooked the chain and slid it free, because out of civic spirit I did not want Miriam found wearing a dead chicken foot either. And I didn't want it touching her.

I didn't want it touching me, for that matter. I put it in her bedside table drawer. Then I went and called 911, and it wasn't any work at all to sound convincingly rattled.

The books have another thing all wrong, too. I'd expected the apartment to be swarming with police just like on "Murder, She Wrote." I got two EMTs and a bored policeman, none of whom cared about my careful, plausible story. We'd had a dinner date. I got here and used my key. I found Miriam.

I lied because even with my limited experience I felt that police do not like to hear about people who find other people dead and just leave, and because if I told the truth they'd probably come down on Lace and Lace already has enough problems. She was going to have some more when I got ahold of her, too.

And if anyone had to pitch an idiot story to the heat, it might as well be me, since I had a number of advantages over Lace. I looked like something I was in most respects: a straight white blue-eyed thirtysomething wage-earner, dressed off the racks of Macy's Herald Square and five foot eight in my stocking feet. Hair the same color I was born with (black), no makeup, no earrings, and no bizarre jewelry out where it could push John Q. Lawdog's buttons. I was highly plausible, in my humble opinion.

But nobody was asking for my opinion this evening, and even the EMTs didn't seem that interested in my story. They zipped Miriam up into a gray plastic mummy bag and wheeled her away. I got out Miriam's phone book for next-of-kin and the policeman copied out her sister Rachel's name and address.

That was it. He made me leave the apartment first and then he took a sign that said NOTICE followed by some type it was too dark in the hallway to read, and put it on the door and told me not to go back in, and that was that.

The police probably wouldn't get around to notifying Rachel Seabrook until at least Monday, he said, if I wanted to call first.

He was nice. I guess he was nice. I'd just found someone I knew dead and lied to the police on top of it and my stomach was full of old scrap iron and I was going to ring Lace's chimes but good and something was *wrong*.

I wanted to cry.

The cop got into his cop car and I went back across the park and down the steps to Broadway. The motorists were still at it—the only thing more dangerous than the subways in New York is the streets—and when I went to put the token in the turnstile at the subway platform I found I was still carrying Miriam's address book in my hands.

Miriam was dead.

"You're so together," Bellflower tells me. Yeah, sure.

I came to New York from the Real World about fifteen years ago. Everybody comes to the Big Apple for something they can't get anywhere else. In my case it was Craft. The One True Polytheism. Wicca.

Unlike a lot of other people I got what I came for.

Miriam was one of the others.

I first met Miriam about five years ago hanging around The Snake—the largest and most out-of-the-broom-closet occult shop on the East Coast. It's been named, at various times, The Naked Truth and The Serpent's Tooth, and is known to its intimates as The Sneaky Snake, or, more briefly, The Snake.

Most of us in what I laughingly call the New York Occult Community, which includes Pagans and Witches and ceremonial magicians and Crowleyites and permutations of all of the above too numerous to catalogue, have been through its doors at one time or another, and about half of us have worked there. It's a nice place to spend Saturday, helping Julian-the-manager with the jewelry inventory and watching the tourists gawk.

Miriam stood out like a sore thumb, striking up bright little conversations with the other browsers in the "Witchcraft and Women's Mysteries" section (Tris, the actual owner, is nothing if not conservative), copying the notices of "Covens Forming" off the bulletin board, and earnestly attending every event the shop offered, from "Enochian Invocation, Calls and Chants" to the Sunday afternoon semi-open Neopagan circles.

I avoided her. The new ones are always trouble, looking for god or guru or someone to tell them the True Facts, and ready to latch onto anyone who will hold still long enough and "Yes, my Lady" her to death.

There are some people in the Community who enjoy that, like Risha the Wonder Witch with her forty-member coven of eternal First Degrees.

I don't. If I had the nerve and the energy to start my own coven, those are the last sort of people I'd pick. They stick forever, they don't learn, and they don't grow. If they wanted to sit in the chorus watching a priest perform, why didn't they stay in the monotheism they came from?

But I digress.

I saw Miriam, and I heard about her (Newbies are an eternal source of gossip. They're so cute when they're dumb), and I met her at just about every "open" event in the city, and we had some conversations and I suggested some books that would probably settle her head on straighter than the moonshine she was reading. Her eyes bugged out when she realized a Real Live Initiate was willing to talk to her and practically oozed down her face when she found out I was entitled to wear the Third Degree silver bracelet and be called "Lady" in A Real Wiccan Circle. Then she got disappointed because I was still a clay-footed human being and wouldn't tell her that what I had was The Answer. Eventually she worked her way through that, too, and forgave me, and we became "sort of" friends.

I even showed her to Bellflower, who is *my* High Priestess, but Miriam wasn't the kind of person who was comfortable with the kind of coven Belle ran, and I sometimes get the feeling that actual religious passion makes Belle nervous.

It's the same old story. Some people just don't manage to click. Every coven is different, and covens with styles that would suit them are full, or gossip of one sort or another ensures they don't get asked when there is an opening, or they just drift away. Score one for the Goddess's winnowing process.

Miriam was one of the ones who drifted. After a year or so on the fringes she gave up on being what she called a "real Witch" when none of the Welsh or Alexandrian or Gardnerian covens would take her and started trying the evanescent trads that spring up and vanish overnight. She even tried Santeria and the O.T.O.—in fact, after a while, every time I saw her she was into something new.

I tried to steer her back toward the safe stuff; that was how she met Lace, shopping the Dianic trads down at Chanters Revel, which was where I was heading now. Lace worked there.

But Miriam hadn't really been "womyn" enough to suit the Dianics. She'd kept looking. Or drifting. And now she was dead. And she had The Answer, if there is a The Answer.

Hard and jagged and unwanted I remembered the chicken claw she'd been wearing around her neck, and I felt a niggling in the part of my brain I reserve for jumping to conclusions. I beat it down because I was not, damn it, a flake like Lace. I'm a charter member of the Conspiracy to Prevent Conspiracy, and I don't look for hidden meanings.

The subway jerked to a stop. The niggle would stay flat for a while. I got off the A at West Fourth Street and started walking toward the Bowery. It was about eight-thirty on a Friday night in June.

Once upon a time a bunch of devout, right-thinking lesbian separatist Goddess-worshipers got fed up with The Sneaky Snake and decided to start their own occult bookstore.

Chanters Revel first opened its doors about five years back, and contrary to conventional wisdom—which is that 50 percent of all new businesses fail every year—is still going strong. They don't cater as much to the dried-bats-and-floorwashes crowd as The Snake does—the

Revel shopper is more likely to be shopping for homeopathic herbs and crystal jewelry, along with the hottest new titles on how to start your own feminist ecosystem. The Revel also brews a mean cup of Red Zinger tea, twenty-five cents and bring your own cup.

I pushed open the door and slid into the shop. For reasons involving rents and overhead, the Revel is located in an area that only the most depraved real estate agent could call SoHo. It's south of Houston, all right—and probably east of the sun and west of the moon as well. It's also one of the few establishments of any sort that has its own herb garden out back.

It was Friday night, and Tollah, who is one-half of Tollah-and-Carrie, the Revel ownership, holds a TGIF Ritual every Friday around nine P.M., East Coast Pagan Time. Which means, in practice, around ten-thirty, but the Friday ritual is mostly for regulars and they don't mind.

The Revel doesn't have indoor ritual space like The Snake does, so Fridays are held in the Revel's little back garden, or with everybody crammed inside if it rains. Tonight was going to be a back garden night, Goddess willing. People were already queuing up to drink quarter-a-cup tea and stand around and gossip.

Tollah waved from the cash register beside the door. I headed for the tea urn. I didn't see Lace anywhere.

I fished my cup out of its hiding place—rank hath its privileges—and dropped a quarter in the box. I poured myself some Zinger. I had a number of reasons for wanting to see Lace, number one or possibly two on the list being that if she'd phoned the police about Miriam before I had and got herself on tape with it, I was probably going to have some really awkward questions to answer eventually.

And for no good reason I wanted to ask Lace why Miriam was wearing a chicken foot around her neck when she died.

I'm not a religious bigot, and I can't have an opinion on something I haven't studied. This leaves me voting "No Award" on a lot of New Age so-called spiritual pathways. Most people are turned off by the Santerios sacrificing chickens to their gods, but exactly how is that different from a kosher butcher slaughtering baby goats for Passover?

Mostly the difference is that the *fleisher* is pulling down $80,000 a year and has a condo in Palm Beach, and the *santero* is on welfare and lives in a fifth-floor walk-up in Queens. Never tell me money doesn't talk. Money's the left-hand path, the ruler of the things of Earth.

So my self-image requires an open mind. Fine. And some gods require blood sacrifices. Fine. It's between them and their worshipers and the legal code of the United States. And some spiritual paths have window dressing that's a real cage-rattler (ever check out Tibetan Buddhism?). This is also fine.

But since all these things were so fine, why was I getting grue and goose bumps because Miriam was wearing a piece of a chicken that the chicken certainly wasn't going to miss now?

Oh, it isn't that I don't believe in evil. It's just that it's rarer than the funny-mentalist tele-vangelists like to think. I prefer to distinguish among evil and stupid and weird. Maybe if I could talk to Lace I could be sure which category Miriam's jewelry fell into.

And maybe I could get some kind of handle on why she was dead. It made no sense. There hadn't been a mark on her that I remembered—not AIDS, not drugs, not terminal cancer—and if she had any medical kinks from diabetes to a bad heart she would have been sure to mention it at some point as proof of her great psychic power. People do.

Miriam Seabrook was dead. For no reason, without even the excuse of traffic accident or urban violence. I wanted to talk the experience to death and bury it in words and the only person I could do that with wasn't anywhere.

If it wasn't unfair, you wouldn't know it was Life.

I poured myself a second cup of tea and tried to distract myself with the bookshelves. There wasn't much there I wanted: I do my book buying at Weiser's or The Snake—my kind of Wicca is too masculinist and hierarchical for the good ladies of Chanters Revel, which is where I do my fraternizing. A foolish consistency is the hobgoblin of little minds, as someone said just after he jumped political parties.

I took one more hopeful look around to see if Lace had come to Earth. It has often been said that a significant percentage of Grateful Dead

groupies make their living by touring the country following the band and selling Grateful Dead
memorabilia to other Grateful Dead groupies
who also make their living by touring the country following the band and . . . You get the idea.
For sheer incestuous symbiosis, Neopagans
have them beat all hollow. Without moving from
my place under a "Women Hold Up Half the Sky"
poster, I could count two occult silversmiths,
one mail-order herbalist, a candlemaker, a guy
who sandblasts mirrors with the holy symbol of
your choice, a pretty good (and very expensive)
astrologer, and a couple people who regularly
read Tarot at The Snake on Wednesdays. It's a
wonder Tollah and Carrie don't go broke—half
the customers at the Revel are their suppliers.

No Lace.

I suddenly realized that I could not face a
TGIF Ritual tonight. Miriam's death didn't belong in it, and I wasn't sure I wanted to tell anybody about that just yet anyway.

I also realized I'd promised Ray I'd finish
those damned galleys still sitting on my board at
work. Before Monday.

Weekends are for sissies.

I decided to circulate a little more in the name
of showing the flag and also to give Lace one last
chance to show up and make me a great excuse
for leaving. I saw everybody else but I didn't see
Lace. Just as the party was starting to move outside—Tollah pulled the shade with the picture
of Mama Kali and the "Closed" sign down over
the glass part of the door—I managed to corner
Carrie.

"Seen Lace?"

Carrie frowned—which made her look cute and ultramundane both and made me wonder yet again what life would be like if I weren't so painfully straight—and made a sincere effort to remember every personal interaction of the last twelve hours.

"She left here about five. She was going to meet that Miriam Seabrook—" Carrie wrinkled her nose in a way that indicated Miriam was Not One Of Us, and from Carrie that was the equivalent of anyone else's screaming phillipic—"and go to that new Greek place to eat. Lace was supposed to bring us back some falafel—but it's okay because Lugh brought in pizza and we split that," she finished in a rush, just in case I might think she was—Goddess avert—mad at Lace.

That settled it. If Carrie said Lace hadn't come back, she hadn't. And in a store that measured ten feet by thirty, someone Lace's size wouldn't exactly be invisible.

"Well, okay," I said, which Carrie could take any way she liked. I went out the back door of the Revel with everyone else, and then down to the bottom of the garden and through the gate and down the alley and out.

And I wondered what Miriam Seabrook, dead space cadet, could possibly have done in life to put that look on gentle Carrie's face.

It was pretty late when I finally got home. New York, you may have heard, is a summer festival: I'd wandered around until I fetched up in front of that bar (you know, the one with no windows and the walls painted black) that seems to be a favorite with all my friends.

Not me. It's not that I mind five bucks for a beer. It's that for that I want light to see and room to drink it afterward.

Despite that, I went in and blew twenty bucks on Tsingtaos until the Real World got to be more irritating than the show I was replaying in my head and I headed for home sweet ungentrified home.

Not that they aren't trying—the gentrifiers, I mean. It was worse back in the eighties when there were still yuppies, but you can feel the hot breath of the real-estate developers panting down your neck six blocks away even now. Let's go co-op! Condo! Loft!

And when there is nothing anywhere on Manhattan Island but studio apartments renting for $1500 a month, they'll say "Where is the charm of the old neighborhoods?"

Sure they will—I don't think. It's the social equivalent of strip mining: They'll be laughing all the way to the bank for the twenty seconds or so it takes their jury-rigged wonderland to turn into slums that'll make Calcutta look like Westchester County, and for the New York economy to crash because nobody but drug lords and lawyers can afford to pay the kind of money that lets people live in places that cost that much.

It's not wanting things like that to happen that leads to block associations (and you thought they were only to stop the spread of crack), and banners across the street saying "Help Save Our Neighborhood," and large informational signs discussing New York City's tax structure as it relates to Alphabet City. And other landmarks of my neighborhood.

Never mind what I pay in rent, or that even if I could afford to live uptown I might not. Think instead about the cultural fallacy that holds that the idea of making money is so sacred that the means by which it is made cannot be questioned—and that anyone saying that sometimes it isn't a good idea to get all the cash profit you possibly can would probably be arrested for heresy if there was a Holy Vehm for the First Church of Money.

When I drink I think too much.

I walked up five flights of stairs and I was home.

The light on my answering machine was blinking as I came in—welcome to the wonderful world of consumer goods. Stupid, but it's my one techno-toy: I can't stand not knowing who wants to talk to me, and since I do a bit of freelance artisting, it's actually a deductible business expense.

I closed the door and flipped the three locks back into place and walked over and pushed the button next to the flashing red light before doing anything else. I have one window and it has no shade; there was enough light to do that by.

The thing obediently played through the part about "leave your name and number after the beep" and got to the point.

"Bast? It's Miriam. Seabrook?"

I am not superstitious, but for a moment I wondered wildly if they had pay phones in the county morgue. But Miriam must have called earlier today, while she was still alive.

Right. Real bright, girl.

"—and I've got to see you," the ghost in the machine went on. "I've really got to see you. It's—" Recorded Miriam drew a shaky breath. I hit "Save" and the tape went back to the beginning and started flashing again.

I went over and turned on the lights. White walls, cracked linoleum, kitchen table old enough to be a Deco-era collectible that isn't. One long room with a bed at the other end and a bathroom with no bath. Home.

And Miriam on my answering machine, person-to-person from the Twilight Zone. Once I played it back she'd be gone for good; the next message coming in would record right over her.

I thought about it for a minute or so, feeling very lucid, and rummaged around until I found my old rinky-dink Sony that I use for taping lectures and stuff. I popped out the tape—music, Sangreal, live, at *Rites of Spring*—and stared at it while my mind helpfully provided the information that there probably wasn't another blank tape in the place and if there were I wasn't in any shape to look for it. So I flipped Sangreal over to Side B and hit "Record" and let it tape a few seconds of my not-too-steady breathing before I went over and hit "Play" on my answering machine again.

Sometimes I just love my life.

"Bast? It's Miriam. Seabrook? I know it's . . . I haven't been in touch, but I've really . . . I need to . . . There's this weird stuff, and I've got to see you. I've really got to see you. It's—" the long pause again, and this time, listening, I could hear tears. "It's too weird. I'm scared. I think they're going to—" The voice stopped abruptly, and when it started again it was bright and upbeat and jarringly fake. "So anyway, call me, okay? Or I'll be down at the Revel, until eleven?"

Clatter of phone hanging up, and then a beep and my message again and Miriam calling back to leave her number. Long hiss of open line, as if she'd waited, not hanging up, hoping I'd come in and pick up the phone and save her. But the answering machine cut her off with a little self-satisfied choodle, and there weren't any other messages on the tape.

I stopped the recorder and rewound the tape and popped it out, and popped the answering machine tape out too, and stuck both of them in a Ziploc Baggie, and put that in a cookie jar that holds subway tokens and incense charcoal and other things that roaches won't eat.

Then I went to bed and tried to convince myself that Miriam's death was from all-natural causes, that Lace's paranoid disappearing act had nothing to do with knowing too much about something, and that Miriam hadn't died as a direct result of being in over her head somewhere.

And I couldn't.

2

My alarm blitzkrieged me out of bed before the sun had come down into my neighborhood, and I was already in the shower before it occurred to me that this was probably Saturday. Further investigation revealed that it was, but by this time I was curious enough to want to try to find out why I'd set my alarm.

Somewhere over the second cup of Morning Thunder I remembered that I had to get back to Houston Graphics and finish that job for Ray. And I might as well call Rachel Seabrook from there while I was at it.

What else I had in mind to do today I wasn't admitting even to me—at least not before breakfast. And maybe lunch.

I got to Houston Graphics about eight and unlocked all the locks I'd locked the night before. I'm not the only one who comes in on weekends—anybody who's worked for the place five years has a set of keys—but if I wasn't the only one today at least I was first. I turned on the lights and the wax machine and the stat camera and the coffeemaker, and when the coffee was ready I poured myself a cup and turned on my light table and settled down to the finicking business of salvaging that type job.

Three hours later—still alone—I straightened up and tried to work the crick out of my lower back. Ray's bitch-kitty of a job was within shouting distance of being done; only another spread to go. And it was late enough so that I could call the time zone next door and be pretty certain I wouldn't wake anyone up.

I didn't want to make that call. How do you tell somebody that their sister is dead? *"Hello, I'm a total stranger and I'm calling to fuck with your head. . . ."* Sure.

I pulled out Miriam's address book. The other numbers in Miriam's book were in every color of the rainbow, decorated with doodles and pentagrams and cryptic notes in massed initials. Rachel Seabrook's number was carefully written in blue-black ink, like a penance. I punched all eleven digits firmly, not giving AT&T a chance to get cute.

Three rings and answer. "Hello?" The authentic Midwest sound of chronic sinus trouble. Area Code 317. Indiana.

"Hello, this is—" I had to think about it for a minute before identifying myself "—Karen Hightower. May I speak to Rachel Seabrook?"

"This is she." Third person peculiar is alive and well in the Middle West.

"I'm afraid I have some bad news for you, Ms.

Seabrook. I'm afraid—" no, I'd said that already "—I'm sorry to tell you. Your sister Miriam is dead."

"How do you know?" Hostile, but not unreasonably so. The telephone is a great leveler. You can't judge what you can't see. All she knew about me was that I knew Miriam.

"I found her body."

There was a pause while we both listened to the long-distance hiss.

"I see. I'm sorry, Miss . . . ?"

"Hightower."

"You must think I'm very cold. But Miriam and I were never close."

"Your number was in her address book. I gave it to the police. They have— She was lying on her bed. She died in her sleep. They should be calling you."

Normally I put sentences together better than that. Grace, wit, charm, adverbs . . . But not today. Death is the only really rude thing anybody can do anymore, it seems. People will forgive rape, murder, theft, and arson, but dying is the unforgivable act. We don't even want to mention anyone crude enough to do it.

"I see. I'm sorry. It must have been very difficult for you. Have you . . . Do you have any idea of what I should do now?" A hesitant laugh: *I'm sorry to be such a bother. . . .*

"I'm sorry," I sorried back, "I don't really know. Maybe the police will be able to tell you. I don't think she had a will. There's her apartment—if you like I could get together her personal papers and send them to you."

That's right, Bast, offer to burgle dead Miriam's apartment for the sister so you have a good excuse.

"I . . . I really can't just drop everything and fly out to New York. We weren't really close." *Tell me it's okay to do it this way. I know I'm supposed to make a big fuss over the dead sister, but this would be easier. Tell me it's all right.*

"If you like I can send you her things."

"Thank you. That would be very kind."

We were never really very close. You might steal everything, but I don't really care. I can say a friend of hers in New York took care of things. We weren't really very close.

"If there is anything you would like. A memento. Please let me know. . . ."

"Thank you, Ms. Seabrook. Let me give you my name and address and phone number. I'll need a UPS address from you."

Thank you. You're very kind. We weren't close. I wrote letters and numbers on my blotter with a technical pen. A rural route in Shelbyville.

By the time I hung up on Rachel Seabrook I had her permission to rummage the length and breadth of Miriam's apartment and strew her worldly goods to the four winds. It was understood that anything with a high resale value would go to Rachel. There wouldn't be much. Not by Shelbyville standards, anyway.

I knew somebody from Shelbyville, Indiana once. He spent so much time being *from* Shelbyville that he never paid much attention to where he actually was. I think he's dead now.

And it was lunchtime, and by now it was obvious even to me how I was going to spend my afternoon. Because Miriam had been afraid when she died, and I wanted to know why.

I finished up the work for Ray, tidied up the studio, and filled in my time sheet. Eloi came in while I was leaving—he was working on a long job, medical textbook with lots of dead babies. He spun his hat the length of the room and made a ringer on the tensor lamp over his board. He didn't say much. He never does. I think he thinks he's Humphrey Bogart but I've never dared ask. At least because he was there I didn't have to lock up again.

I caught the Uptown train. When I got to Miriam's apartment I took the police notice off the door and used Lace's keys to get in. Crime number one.

Inside, the place looked and smelled like an abandoned hotel room. I had a flash of Stephen King–land cyanotic zombies shambling out of closets, which was stupid. Death is a part of life. If the dead interact with the living at all (insufficient data), it is not reasonable to think that they will be any more antisocial than they were while they were alive. Miriam had been my friend, sort of, and anything else on a day-trip from Between The Worlds I could deal with.

Meanwhile, here was a quick introduction to Death, Twentieth Century–style. You die, and two weeks later the landlord rents your apartment. Everything you scraped to buy or collect is

suddenly worthless, and all people can think of
is how to get rid of it gracefully.

There's something to be said for the old custom of funerary goods. One big bonfire and all
the fuss would be over.

I opened the windows and put on the kettle.
Miriam's purse was still on the microscopic fold-
down Conran's kitchen table. I left it there and
rummaged around a little until I found about
what I expected: two joints wrapped in foil in
the freezer compartment of the fridge and half
a Baggie of magic mushrooms in a recycled
Skippy jar in the cupboard next to the vervain.
The Sixties are alive and well and living in the
Craft in New York City.

I threw the 'shrooms and the pot into the
trash and hoped there wasn't anything worse
around—and if there was, that I'd recognize it.
The vervain went, too—not that it's illegal; it's
a harmless herb used in a lot of Wiccan and
Pagan banishing rituals. On the other hand, I
only had Miriam's word for it that the gray-green
stuff in the jar marked "Vervain" was vervain
and not, say, oregano.

The tea-water boiled while I finished denud-
ing the kitchen of occult and counterculture ad-
ditives. The stuff that was legal, semimundane,
easily identifiable, and still useful I left lined up
on the counter for later collection. Then I took
my tea out to the living room.

I'd never been in Miriam's apartment before
last night. Whatever her day job was she'd made
decent money on it or had outside financial
help; this place probably rented for between six

and seven hundred a month. I wondered if there was any way on earth to collect her security deposit for Shelbyville.

It was a typical New York apartment: kitchen on the right, bathroom behind it down a hall, bedroom opening off the hall, and living room straight ahead.

The living room looked like everybody else's I hung out with. Not much here to excite Shelbyville: the couch was a curbside rescue, the end tables were wooden crates, the coffee table was an old trunk. The room was a first-class job of urban scavenging, but the standards of Fly-Over Country are not our own. All Rachel Seabrook would see was junk.

Across from the couch was the standard brick and board bookcase, with the standard authors: Adler, Valiente, the Farrars, Buckland. Some Crowley, and even a copy of the Sumerian-style *Necronomicon* somebody published as a stunt a few years back. It's a complete grimoire of Sumerian magic, all right, but it doesn't contain any banishing rituals. The system was written without them, and so it's worthless. Who ever heard of drawing without an eraser?

Records and tapes, all harmless. A pile of magazines: *Gnostica* and *Green Egg* and *Fireheart*. A few copies of *Ms.* and *Mother Jones*, for variety.

Copies of *The White Goddess* and *The Golden Bough*, both paperback and full of Miriam's marginal notes. But nothing here you couldn't show your mother, if your mother happened to be Sybil Leek.

On the right-angle wall there was another, lower, bookcase that had her altar on it. Most Pagans have one—it's just a flat surface, sometimes covered with a cloth, where you keep chatchkis that are meaningful to you. Light a candle, burn some incense, reaffirm your personal belief system.

Like everything else in the room, Miriam's could have been issued stock from Pagan Central Supply: A blue pillar candle, an incense burner, some big quartz crystals, a Goddess figure. Hers was a museum shop replica of the Goddess of the Games, from Crete.

The little Goddess was dusty, and so was the top of the candle. Well, we aren't any of us demon housekeepers. To coin a phrase.

But the coffee table wasn't dusty. Neither were the tapes piled on the bookshelf. So Miriam did clean.

But not her altar. Not even so much as you'd expect from handling the things—lighting the candle, and so on.

Theory: Miriam hadn't been near her altar in weeks.

Miriam, if you can hear me, the next time I see you I'm going to thump your punkin' haid in. What the hell were you up to?

The answer, of course, was in the bedroom.

I felt the energy as soon as I crossed the threshold. It's not a particularly witchy trick—you do it all the time: Ever walk into a room full of people and *know* a fight's in progress? Or come home, and not even bother to give a yell because you *know* there's nobody there? Maybe you don't talk about things like that, but Witches do, and we have to call the reason-for-knowing something. So we call it energy, most of us. Whatever it is, it's the thing that changes.

The energy in Miriam's room was not good. I thought about Stephen King again. But I'd been here yesterday and the only energy I'd felt was Miriam being dead.

This was not that.

I went back out to the living room and stopped at Miriam's dusty altar. There were matches on a lower shelf. I lit the candles and got out the charcoal. I couldn't find any incense around the altar, but I'd seen some in the kitchen.

I went back in and came out with a self-seal Baggie of something that looked like coarse sand. The grains were red, yellow, and black. I'd saved it because I knew what it was. Russian Church incense—the heavy smoky stuff, all copal and frankincense and myrrh. It made a nice familiar smell as the smoke made Jacob's Ladders up to the ceiling. The little Goddess seemed to shine brighter, as if she liked being remembered. And I knew that nothing bad could get at me while She watched.

Most adults lose that sense of serenity, the idea that somebody else is going to shoulder the load and do the looking-out-for. Maybe wives had it before Women's Lib, when Hubby took all the heat, or maybe that's another myth of the Golden Age that there's no way to check. But it's one of the things that religion has always promised to provide.

Not, mind, that I'm going to leave my door unlocked and expect the Great Goddess to keep the muggers away. She encourages independence.

But I felt better now.

I went back into the bedroom and opened the window, and a bunch of Austrian crystal suncatchers that Shelbyville might like went spinning. They sent little light-flies spinning over the walls that Miriam had lovingly painted with a pastoral landscape in shades of violet, and wickedness popped like a bubble.

I'd known Miriam was a wannabe artist as well as a wannabe Witch. I hadn't known she had this much talent. It made her death worse, somehow, which is unfair.

I looked around. Mattress on a platform. One nightstand a salvage job with a drawer, the other one of those cheap metal footlockers from Lamston's. There were another two footlockers at the foot of the bed.

Bedside lamps—cheap copies of Art Nouveau. You used to be able to buy them down at the Canal Street Flea Market. Mirror (cracked) and discard-chest of drawers, a gift of the Garbage Goddess, painted lavender and decorated with painted vines. A straight chair and a square hassock, also secondhand.

The closet, as always, was tiny, narrow, and deep. It held sneakers, Tibetan tie-dye vests, and one or two suits of mundane clothes that had that indefinable look of being a couple of years out of style. For the second time today I wondered what Miriam did for a living. There wasn't enough in the way of "straight" clothes here for a work wardrobe. Of course, maybe she had a job like mine, in which case they wouldn't care if she showed up naked, so long as she got the work done.

But Miriam wasn't going to be working anymore. Miriam was dead.

Why?

And what had left that bogeymonster feeling in the room?

The actual cause of death in every case is the same: The heart stops. What coroners call the proximate cause is *why* the heart stops. Miriam was young (thirtysomething), not overweight by more than a few pounds, in fair-to-good physical condition, and if she was seeing Lace she was certainly watching what she ate—Lace is a combat vegetarian. From the way she'd looked when I found her I ruled out those nineties charmers, AIDS and cocaine.

Which left what?

Forget it, Bast. Lots of people die of lots of things.

Poison, for example.

But that would make it suicide, unless Lace had killed her.

"There's this weird stuff, and I've got to see you."

And I didn't think someone who'd left a message like that on my answering machine would kill herself a few hours later. She'd meant to be at the Revel's TGIF. She'd said so.

I went back to the closet and did a thorough job this time. Nothing but clothes, nothing in the pockets. A standard-issue black polyester ritual robe like The Snake sells. Miriam—or somebody—had embroidered it all around the yoke, hem, and sleeves. Silk thread. I took it out and laid it on the bed.

The top of the dresser was covered with more of the usual stuff: New Age cosmetics from the Revel and elsewhere, half a dozen bottles of essential oils. Hairbrush, earrings, bracelet, watch, ring. Little ceramic Ho-Tei with his fat celadon belly.

The top drawer of the dresser held more jewelry, some unopened mail, and a passbook and checkbook from Chemical with the ATM card stuck in the passbook. A set of numbers that I was betting was Miriam's access code was written on the card in gold ink—and, damn it, they tell you and *tell* you not to do that.

She had about two hundred in checking and nearly a thousand in savings, no recent withdrawals. Her last paycheck was also in the drawer, already endorsed. I made a note to deposit it. I also took out Miriam's address book and made a note in the back: Chastain Designs, up on West 47th. The Diamond District, for you out-of-towners.

Nobody calls West 47th "Diamond and Jewelry Way," just as nobody calls Sixth Avenue the "Avenue of the Americas." We started with numbers and we'll stay with them. Or maybe numbers are just easier to spell.

At least the paycheck explained Miriam's lifestyle. Chastain Designs—I knew from my Saturdays at The Snake—was a wholesale jeweler;

from the hourly rate on Miriam's paycheck she did some kind of scut work—probably assembly—that netted her about enough to pay her rent and utilities without too much left over. Assembly-line jewelers aren't paid a lot—they're just hired hands—but if Miriam was doing any freelancing at all she could be making good money. Could have been.

I wondered if she did design. If she did, it was a good bet she'd asked the Revel to handle some of her pieces on consignment. I wondered if Carrie'd turned her down.

I started a second pile on the bed: Jewelry, bank stuff. I put the paid bills and the letters on top of the ritual robe. Triage. After a minute I opened the nightstand and added the chicken foot to the robe pile.

One of the lockers at the foot of the bed held correspondence. Miriam kept everything. There were copies of Pagan newsletters and flyers for festivals and membership applications for groups and catalogs and, occasionally, personal correspondence with members of this group or that. There was no insurance except an on-again-off-again policy with Blue Cross that didn't seem to be on right now.

My tea got cold while I read through the antique mail, and after an hour or so I had an empty footlocker, a full wastebasket, two more neat piles, and an urge to raid Miriam's kitchen.

You get to know the groups that are taking the risk of going public. I recognized all the names from their notices in the back of all the Pagan newsletters that Miriam got and I get, too.

All innocent. All mainstream (for Neopaganism). Nothing here that could explain the look on Carrie's face last night at the Revel when she mentioned Miriam. Gentle Carrie, who never wanted to say anything bad about anybody.

I went off to the kitchen and made more tea and a sandwich and congratulated myself that Miriam didn't have a cat. If she did I'd probably end up adopting it, and I didn't want to do that.

Don't get me wrong. I like cats; what Witch doesn't? (Although, if you want to get technical, the historic and traditional familiar for practitioners of northwest European–based non-Christian religion traditions is the toad, because the English garden toad secretes the same hallucinogen—bufotenin—when upset as that found in Carlos Casteneda's favorite mushroom, *Amanita muscaria*—which is why so many ancient potions call for toad sweat as one of their ingredients.)

But I digress. The trouble with cats versus me is that cats, like all animals, are looking for something. Their range. The other members of their pack. A warm spot in the sun. Company. Locking a cat up alone for twelve hours a day in a coffin-shaped and coffin-sized apartment is not my idea of giving an animal these things.

Stewardship is a pretty outmoded word these days, but if you love something—or even if it just belongs to you—you take care of it, right?

Anyway, I was glad Miriam didn't have a cat.

While I ate I went through her purse. Wallet first. Miriam had a Macy's card, a secured Visa, a New York Public Library card, and was a mem-

ber of the Park Terrace East Neighborhood
Watch and her building's tenant association
and Greenpeace.

Everything so normal it hurt. I kept digging.
It was a big purse.

More letters. I made a note to write all these
people and tell them why Miriam wasn't going to
be writing anymore. A pair of Chastain Designs
earrings still on their showcard—very upmar-
ket. A candy bar. More nameless keys. Wallet,
paperback, comb, hand mirror, Tarot cards
(Waite design), stubs of a couple candles, Ziploc bag of granular incense. I opened it and
sniffed. More Russian Church incense.

And down at the bottom, the paydirt I didn't
want to find. A little brown book.

In the olden days, around 1500 C.E. (Christian Era), most books were this size. In modern
days, A.X. (after xerographic replication), lots of
books are this size again. The *Book Of The Law*,
say, or *The Sayings of Chairman Mao*. The size of
an 8½ × 11 sheet of paper, cut in fourths.

The book in Miriam's purse, however, had
never seen the light of copier, Xerox or other-
wise.

It was, as previously intimated, about four by
five. It was a thin book, maybe a quarter of an
inch thick, and the front cover was much thicker
than the back—maybe half the total thickness.
The book was bound in pale grainy leather—pig-
skin, maybe. The covers and spine were blank,
but it had the look of a professional binding job.

I opened it. The inside front cover was thick
because it had a thin sheet of painted wood

bound into it: color on black, and the colors faint and hard to see. It reminded me of an icon, but their backgrounds are gold.

Got it. Russian lacquerwork. There used to be a display of it up at the Crabtree & Evelyn in Citicorp Center, and Brentano's (when there was a Brentano's) used to carry it. Gorgeous stuff, fabulously expensive and all done in the traditional manner, right down to the final polish with a wolf's tooth.

I wondered if this piece I was holding had been polished with a wolf's tooth.

Had Miriam gone bonkers and converted to the Eastern Orthodox Church?

I flipped through the book.

The first page said: "Khazar Wicca—Invokations" (sic), in fake-medieval illumination. The rest of the pages were plainer, but they were all hand-done, calligraphed in brown ink. I recognized Miriam's penmanship from the samples I'd seen in her bedroom. Every few pages there was a large four-color initial; the last two were just pencil ghosts and their pages were blank. The book seemed to be a series of poems or prayers (or even, as the title almost said, invocations), with the occasional word in a different alphabet lettered painstakingly in. I read what I could.

As I have said before and will continue to say, I know just about enough about the history of worship on this planet not to judge religions on the basis of their window dressing and not enough to judge them in spite of it. Religious art

consisting of pictures of horrible tortures and a
liturgy celebrating blood and slaughter does not
mean that the priests or congregation of said
religion intend anything similar. Case in point:
the modern Catholic Church, whose dogma
would be truly hair-raising if you thought they
meant any of it. Or the Tibetan Buddhists, some
of the gentlest people I know, despite their *raok-
shas.*

Having said that, I proceeded to judge Miriam's latest religion on precisely that basis. Because it was calling itself Wicca, and there are
some things that are simply not Wiccan. Any
spiritual path that celebrates them, and calls
itself Wicca anyway, is doing so with intent to
deceive. And a religion that starts out lying to
you about what it is isn't likely to be healthy for
seekers and other living things.

The poems were all about death. Not death as
an inevitable and sometimes frightening stage
in the Great Cycle of Rebirth, but death as an
end in itself—something to be celebrated.

And the death the poems were celebrating
was the planet's.

*"When winter comes forever and the dream of
green is gone—"*

*"Black sky bleak with no stars rising, where
the sun is found no more—"*

*"Come, Wintermother, bring an end to all that
lives—"*

The literary level was about what you'd expect—rather silly rewarmed Kipling—but the
subtext was spooky and nasty. This was one ar-

tifact that wasn't going to make its way back to Shelbyville.

Before I closed it I took one last look at the icon. Someone other than Miriam had done the work on it, trying hard to fake a traditional lacquerwork style. Now that I knew what to expect I could make out the design, but somehow the poems had more power. In a world where the *Nightmare on Elm Street* movies are light entertainment, visual images no longer have the power to shock. Two monsters—one red, one blue—tearing a naked woman in half in the middle of a blasted heath was strictly amateur hour.

Except for one thing.

The tiny painted woman was recognizably Miriam. And she was wearing something around her neck. It was a yellowish blob, at this size. Maybe a chicken foot.

Oh, Miriam, you stupid git, I told you and told you the things to look out for. These woods are dark and dangerous, and in them lurk lots of people whose only interest is in being worshiped.

Sad but true, and at least now Miriam was free to try again, which didn't make me feel a whole lot better, to tell the bedrock truth. I wondered if Lace knew anything about the group Miriam had been with; it would be good to put the word out on them as being people to avoid. I finished my sandwich, picked up the book and purse, and started back into the bedroom.

The phone rang.

I debated whether to answer it through six rings. It was unlikely it was the New York Police calling to see if any housebreakers were home,

and nobody else knew that Miriam was dead—
unless Lace had mentioned it, which, knowing
Lace, was unlikely. It might even be for Miriam—
or at worst it might be Rachel Seabrook, checking to see if I was here. At any rate, answering
the phone could not get me in more trouble than
I was in now. I thought.

I picked up the phone in the middle of a ring.
"Hello?"

There was a —choke? —cough? —gasp of
surprise? from the other end of the line.

"Holy shit! It's Miriam! She's—" There was a
loud hang-up and then a dial tone in my ear.

I stared at the phone meditatively. Adult
male voice, slight boroughs accent. Not expecting the phone to be answered by Miriam in a big
way.

Because he'd killed her?

You've been reading too many murder mysteries, Bast. Nobody killed Miriam—and if they
had, why would her killer be phoning to tell her
about it?

Because he'd poisoned her and wanted to see
if it had worked?

Unfortunately that was too plausible for my
peace of mind. The fact that I'd managed to give
him one hell of a scare did little to compensate
for the fact that now he—my mythical murderer—would be looking for Miriam to finish the
job.

But Miriam Had Not Been Murdered.

If she had been, would the police notice?

And why, on the basis of, let's face it, no evidence at all, was I so convinced someone had killed her?

I didn't know.

So I did the first sensible thing I'd done since yesterday. I called Bellflower.

Lady Bellflower, to give her her proper liturgical title, is the High Priestess (HPS for short) of my coven, Changing, and has been in the Witch business longer than I have. She's short, round like the Venus of Willendorf is round, has exophthalmic baby blue eyes and frizzy ash-blond hair that is usually standing out in all directions. Like most of our native New York Crafters, Belle comes from a Jewish humanist background, got fed up with the mancentricity of Judaism, and went looking for the Goddess. If you'll read the Old Testament (Jeremiah 44:15–19), you'll see this is not the first time Jews have gone looking for the Lady.

Belle took her training a generation or so out from the original Long Island Coven. The Long Island Coven was founded in the early sixties by an American couple named Rosemary and Raymond Buckland, who were trained by Gerald Gardner in England. I'm Gardnerian lineage; since Belle is the one who trained me, so is she. But after running a traditional Gardnerian coven for over a decade (a wonder in itself when the median burnout time for leadership in the Community is about five years), Belle decided to take a more eclectic approach to life. This has made her something of a scandal in the strictly Gardnerian part of the Community. It also makes her one of the few Witches with her own weekly radio show on WBAI.

I call Belle's approach the New Hope of the Craft. She laughs, but it's ecumenicism that's going to carry us into the next century. If you think that's a good idea, you'd like Belle.

The phone rang several times and I sat through the "leave your name and number" message that Belle uses to screen her calls.

"This is Bast," I said after the beep. "Belle? You there? Okay; today is Saturday, June 16, it's around three—"

"Bast?" Belle's voice has two registers: basso profundo and squeak. To save time she uses both together.

"Hi. Look, you got a minute for me to dump my problems on you? A friend of mine is dead. You remember Miriam Seabrook—"

Belle is a good listener; it didn't take me long to unload the last twenty-four hours. I left in Lace and her phone call but left out the Khazar chicken-foot conspiracy, for reasons I wasn't quite sure of at the time.

"Do you want us to do a Crossing for her?" Belle asked when I finished.

Crossing is short for Crossing Over; I understand the Witches borrowed the term from the Spiritualists, though most of us won't admit it now. Most Neopagans (who borrowed it from us Witches) believe that after death people go to a paradise (which most of us call the Summerland, another Spiritualist borrowing) to rest, relax, and make plans for their next incarnation, in which most of us also believe.

Sure it sounds stupid, but try explaining Christian heaven with a straight face ("You die, see, and then you get to wear wings, and a halo, and a long white robe. And they give you this harp. And then you stand around a giant glowing throne, singing. Forever. That's right. No, you don't do anything else. When you're dead you *want* to sing.")

Anyway, Crossing Over is about sending good thoughts and good energy to the person currently on their way to the Summerland. At worst it's harmless and does what all good funerals do, which is comfort the living. At best, well, that depends on your belief system, doesn't it?

So: "Yeah, sure. That'd be good. When?"

"Well, Changing's meeting next Friday anyway. Why don't you just pass the word; I'll make it an open circle."

Open means that any friendly person can attend, regardless of affiliation. Most of Changing's circles aren't exactly closed, but guests generally have to be cleared with the Priest/ess of Importance for the Rite; usually Bellflower.

"Yeah. Thanks. Lace'll want to be there. Damn it, Belle, how could Miriam go and do a shit thing like that—she was thirty-two and she just dropped dead!"

I was crying, to my utter astonishment. Belle just hung on the other end of the electronic umbilical and let me snivel. I mopped my eyes on my sleeve and did counted-breathing exercises.

"Who's making arrangements for the mundane funeral?" Belle asked after a while.

"Damned if I know. I think there's an autopsy. It'd have to be after that. Her sister is from Indiana, and not exactly wild to do much of anything. So I guess there's not going to be any funeral."

"Yes there is," Belle said firmly. "Ours. Look, why don't you come on up after you're done there? You're only a few blocks away."

"Yeah. Okay. Maybe. Look— Thanks."

Belle sighed, the way she does when she suspects she is not getting through to someone. "Blessed be, Bast."

"B-B, my Lady. Ta."

I hung up and went into the bathroom and did a better job of drying and cleaning my face than my sleeve could provide. I splashed cold water on it and looked in the mirror. Same old white-bread wonder Witch. My eyes were living refutation of the fact that blue and red make purple. I looked like a cross between the American flag and an albino raccoon with leprosy.

Bellflower says that the reason I haven't left Changing is because I can't find any trainees who would be up to the standards she says I'd set for any coven I ran. She says I'd rather go along with the familiar even if I disagree with it (we've had discussions about how Changing is run) than put my own ideas out on the line and be forced to change them. She says that I'll be a happier, healthier, calmer person when I stop feeling that there is one right way to do anything, especially in Wicca.

Maybe. Maybe there isn't one right way. But there are a lot of ways that are demonstrably better than a lot of other ways, and there are some ways (Belle and I differ on this) that are just plain wrong.

Had I been the wrong kind of friend for Miriam? Had I spent so much time insisting that she find the right path in the right way that I steered her away from all the almost-as-goods right down the one she died in?

Or (admit it to yourself, Bast), died *of*?

Okay, it was a stupid idea. But dead didn't have to mean murdered. Hundreds of people die of Christian Science every year, and it isn't called murder. Or even suicide. If Miriam's current spiritual path had included eating things out of boxes marked "Not To Be Taken Internally," it would explain her death. And any competent, responsible, or at least cautious guru would have stopped her—if he could and if he knew.

I wanted to find out who Miriam's guru was. And if he *had* known. And if he was a responsible person.

And, bottom line, I wanted to find out just how much guilt I ought to cop to.

I went back to finish rousting Miriam's personal possessions. I figured I'd give Lace first pick of the stuff and then the rest could go to her friends and mine on a first-come basis. Everything that Shelbyville was likely to want was already piled on the bed—I didn't think that the arrival of three crates of books on Witchcraft and Paganism would make Rachel Seabrook's life any happier.

I found Miriam's altar tools, the ones she'd use to set up a circle. I found her personal workbooks, all crammed full of dreams, rituals, poems.

What I didn't find was her *athame*.

Remember that old Dorothy L. Sayers mystery where Lord Peter, arriving on the scene of the crime, is dead certain it's murder because he cannot find the one thing that absolutely, positively, *must* be there in the kit of a working artist?

This was like that. There is one thing that almost every Witch and Pagan has—and a wannabe conservative like Miriam certainly would have. In fact, I knew she had one, because I gave it to her myself.

There was a knife-smith named Ironshadow who was in the Community a while back doing all the local Pagan festivals and Society for Creative Anachronism events. Ironshadow had a nice line in inexpensive ritual daggers—*athames*—that had about a six-inch double-edged blade, ebony-wood handle, and your choice of decorator pommels.

I'd bought one for Miriam after hearing her whine for two hours about that hoary old piece of Craft folklore that says you can't buy your own ritual blade, it must be given to you by a friend. We'd both been at Panthea Festival. Ironshadow's table had been right there. The one I picked had an amber pommel. I'd always felt guilty about how happy it made her. She didn't see the meanness in the gesture at all.

Was that what my tie was to Miriam? Guilt?

Anyway, she took it back to Ironshadow and had him engrave her magical name—Sunshrike—around the pommel-bezel, and he signed the blade up near the tang, and I'd know it anywhere.

Except it wasn't anywhere. And it had to be.

I turned the place inside out in good earnest this time, looking for every place a paranoid ex-hippie might hide the most precious thing she had, the thing that symbolized her spirit—the thing that *was*, in occult terms, Miriam/Sunshrike. The phone rang again while I was looking and nearly stopped my heart, but it was only Belle, wondering where I was.

"Uh, it's going to take me longer than I thought to finish up here. Why don't we just give it a miss?"

"You're still coming Thursday?"

Thursday was Midsummer, one of the Eight Great Sabbats In the Wheel Of The Year. It would be Just Family—all the members of Changing who would manage to juggle work and world to get there.

"I'm still coming Thursday," I said, as much to the Goddess on Miriam's altar as to Belle.

By seven o'clock I was starving, and I knew for a fact that Miriam's *athame* was not in the place. Where it was if it wasn't here was a nagging question that didn't manage to seem too urgent, at least on this empty a stomach. After all, Miriam was dead. Her *athame* didn't matter to her now.

Did it?

I gathered up my two piles. Rachel's went into an old suitcase I'd found. Mine went part in my purse, part bundled into Miriam's ritual robe and lashed together with her belt cord.

I made a fast circuit of the apartment to make sure everything was tidy for extended absence—closed the windows, stripped the soiled bed (afterthought), doused the candles and the incense on the altar.

The Goddess looked at me, and I picked her up and put her in my purse, taking off the scarf I was wearing to wrap her in.

Good-bye, Miriam. I guess you might have been a better friend than I thought.

And I was a worse one.

3

I'd meant to go down to Chanters Revel and see if Lace'd ever turned up, but going through Miriam's apartment wiped me out worse than I thought. I got home about eight-thirty Saturday night and there were, thank God-or-Goddess, no messages on the answering machine. So I lay down for half an hour and when I woke up it was about five in the morning. So I did what any sensible person would do: turned over and went back to sleep.

The next time I woke up it was to the sound of my own voice telling somebody to leave their name and number and I would get back to them. Lace was starting to do just that when I grabbed the phone.

"Lace? It's me." Which is a damned stupid thing to say when answering your own phone, but answering machines do that to people.

"I thought I better call you." Lace sounded like she had a major head cold—or like she'd been crying for a long time.

"I think you'd better talk to me, Lace. Did you call the police Friday?"

"No." Defiantly.

Well, that was one weight off my mind—assuming Lace was telling the truth.

"Look, you know where I live. Come on up and I'll fix you a cuppa. And I've got some of Miriam's things for you."

Lace foghorned something unintelligible and hung up. But she'd come. Getting Miriam's things would get Lace here. She didn't have Miriam's keys anymore. I had two sets now—Lace's and Miriam's—and at the moment I could see no good reason to give Lace either one.

I piled the jewelry I'd earmarked for Lace on the table and set the tea-water to boil.

For a wonder in our neck of the woods, Lace is actually Lace's real name. Georgina Lacey Devereaux, from some place down South before she came here to the Big Empty. You can't tell where she's from by the way she talks—unless she gets really mad, when it comes out in her swearing.

Lace is actually an inch shorter than I am, but she gives the impression of being really big, in that broad-shouldered, husky, breastless way some dykes get. Her hair is cut I-dare-you short and bleached-out white: in her army surplus, spikes, and leather she looks like a cheap Rutger Hauer clone from *Bladerunner*.

When I looked through the door at her her eyes were so red and swollen she reminded me of one of those white mice the government spends millions giving cancer to in an attempt to prove that nicotine may be harmful. I popped my locks and let her in.

"Want a drink?" I said. Ten-fifteen in the morning. But she stopped looking so hostile. I put the tequila and the orange juice on the table.

"No harm done, Lace. It was real heavy, okay?"

She smiled at me and began to cry, so I turned away and started working on what would be scrambled eggs and tofu with red pepper. Lace assembled most of the working parts of a Tequila Sunrise and made it go away.

Like I said, Lace is a vegetarian. Distilled vegetables are her favorite kind.

When I'd reached the point of charring some bagels in my toaster oven, Lace had reached the point where she was poking through the jewelry.

"I called her sister Rachel," I said. "She asked me to pack up Miriam's things, so I went up there yesterday and went through all her stuff. I'm sending Rachel the official papers and bank things, and some of the jewelry. I thought you'd want these, and if there's anything else in Miriam's apartment you think maybe somebody could use, I don't think Rachel's going to mind."

Breakfast was ready. We ate eggs. Lace piled the pieces of jewelry on each other. I'd packed the gold for sending back to Shelbyville, along with the most mundane of the silver pieces. This was the snake ring and ax earring stuff—and a pentacle I'd found tossed in the back of a drawer, as if Miriam'd found something better.

"There was this thing she used to wear around her neck," Lace said. "Where's that?"

It was in a Ziploc Baggie with the Khazar book, but I wasn't going to tell Lace that. Lace is the violent type. "Where's what? She wasn't wearing anything." I was gambling, just a bit, that Lace wouldn't remember too clearly her last sight of Miriam.

Lace frowned. "She always wore it. It was . . . It was like this rabbit's foot, only a bird."

If I'd never seen Miriam's pendant, I'd never have recognized it from Lace's description.

"She wasn't wearing it? You're sure?"

Lace sounded more upset than seemed reasonable over the absence of a piece of jewelry.

"I checked the place over before I called the cops. No ritual jewelry on her, and nothing out in plain sight in the apartment. What was Miriam into lately, Lace?"

"Why?"

Lace had been mellowing out under the combined influence of tequila, sympathy, and my respect for the fine art of paranoia. Now she looked wary.

"Well, you know, I kind of got the feeling that Carrie didn't want Miriam around the Revel anymore, and Changing is having a Crossing Over for her next Friday, and I didn't know whether to tell them down there. . . ."

"Damn that Carrie bitch." The words came out flat and evenly spaced, with no inflection. "She never did like Miriam. She was always going on about how Miri had to make a commitment—and then when she did, Carrie just couldn't hack it. Miriam was always more C.M. than she was," Lace added plaintively.

I could believe that. C.M. is Community shorthand for Ceremonial Magic—or Magick, if you prefer. C.M. is mostly Christianity-based, hierarchical, sexist, and very expensive to practice. From what I'd seen in Miriam's apartment, Lace didn't mean it literally—except that the Khazar book I'd seen had a whole lot more in common with Ceremonial Magic than with Wicca.

"Well, you know, Infinite Diversity in Infinite Combinations," I said. The First Church of Star Trek has a lot to answer for. "What did you think of Miriam's group when you met them?"

"I didn't meet them. She wouldn't take me. She said they weren't very out—of the broom-closet, you know—and real hetero. She was pretending she was straight."

Lace's mouth made a shape you usually only see on tragedy masks—and no wonder, if her lover had decided to join a homophobic group. Miriam must have had to work like hell to find one, too; the trendy phobia on the New Aquarian Frontier is hetero.

I made encouraging noises, but Lace wanted to forget the whole thing and I didn't get much. Miriam'd found her new group about three months ago. Lace didn't remember its name, but thought it was called "something like Baklava." Once she was in, Miriam dropped most of her other Community contacts. In the first flush of conversation she said some things about the group—and against some others—that got Tollah and Carrie's back hair up. Some hard words about collaboration and party-Paganism were said.

"I'm sure they'll want to know about the Crossing Over anyway," I said soothingly. I wondered what Miriam could possibly have said to make Carrie hold a grudge for three months. I'd probably have to die ignorant; Carrie'd never tell.

Lace finished her second or maybe third spiked orange juice and had tea, and I wrote out all the information about the Crossing Over on a 3 × 5 card to post down at the Revel. I changed my mind and gave Lace one of the sets of Miriam's keys—how much trouble could she get into in an empty apartment?—and we made a date to get together about the stuff in Miriam's apartment—maybe next Saturday, the 23rd, before the rent that Miriam wasn't around to pay anymore was due. Then she left.

After Lace was gone I made myself another cup of tea and got out the stuff I'd taken from Miriam's apartment. That reminded me about the little Goddess, so I got her out, too, and unwrapped her and put her on my own altar. She wasn't displacing anybody; I figured she'd get along with my thunderstone just fine.

She looked a lot brighter here than she had at Miriam's, all gold and ivory (although considering where she came from, it was probably cast resin and gilt paint). Goddess of the Games, Lady of the Wild Things, Maid and Mother but never Bride.

There are some people who think I have an overromantic imagination.

I picked up the rest of the stuff and put it on the table.

Ritual robe. Four 8 × 10 blank books that were Miriam's occult diaries. The Khazar prayer book. The chicken-foot necklace.

No *athame.* That still bothered me. And I didn't know why.

Even assuming that Miriam had, as I was starting to think, gotten involved in a really coercive power-tripping occult group calling itself (with no justification) a Wiccan coven, what that was, was sad. Not a case for Denny Colt, aka The Spirit, superhero investigator.

So why was I trying to make Miriam's death into a crime with a victim and a victor?

Tidiness, probably. Man is the pattern-making animal; the idea that some things Just Happen offends us. If Miriam died, it had to be for cause. Even murder was better than a random cosmos.

It is thinking like that which has led to most of the witch hunts of history. Sometimes things *do* Just Happen—if you're of a philosophical bent, call it a part of the Lady's pattern that's just too big for you to see. But stop looking for a villain, Bast.

Right? Right. Good advice.

And in order to take it I wanted to find out more about "Baklava," alias the Khazar Tradition. Maybe they didn't use *athames.* Maybe Miriam had broken hers, or lost it, or given it away.

Sure.

I glanced through the diaries just enough to

put them in chronological order, then started going through them in good earnest. Accounts of dreams, bad poetry, artwork never meant for anyone else to see.

Miriam wasn't a diligent archivist, but enough of the entries were dated for me to be able to figure out what was going on. Every few pages the same entry, some variation of: "This time I think I've found It, The Answer. . . ." and then a flurry of pages done in the style of her newest find. Over and over, for three books and four years. Miriam never changed. She never stopped looking for an answer that came from outside, that she could lace on like a corset to make her life the right shape. She didn't learn anything from all the "The Answer"s that turned out not to be.

We bring the answer with us. All the traditions, all the paths, teach us to see what is already here. That is the central Mystery of our Mystery that I had never convinced Miriam of. The secret is that there is no secret.

The fourth book started in spring of this year. Miriam was still using the dating style of her last fling, so the year appeared to be seven thousand something and the date was 28 Inanna, but after that she started talking about the vernal equinox, so I knew it was March 21. It started out as a series of dreams—ice and snow images—and then, rare for Miriam, an actual diary entry:

"Dark Moon Waxing." (That would make it around March 28. I consulted my pocket ephemeris to be sure.) "Tonight I met a Man of Great

Power. He was at The Snake, and he says that he was looking for *me* because he heard me *calling* him—"

The trouble with lines like these, that were old when snake oil was new, is that they are also literally true. The urge that makes you pick up the phone and call a long-lost friend who, it turns out, was thinking about you—what is that, if not what Miriam was describing?

Coincidence? Thank you, no. If I believed in magic as hard as some people believe in random chance and coincidence, by now I would have walked off a building thinking I could fly. But you don't have to believe in something to use it. No one ever had to believe in a chair, you'll notice. Some things are, some things aren't. Use your five sound senses and any more you may have been given, can develop, or encourage. And make up your own mind, not somebody else's.

Here endeth the lecture. So far the only thing wrong with the Mysterious Stranger was that it's bad manners to say these things (even if true) to total strangers. I went on with my reading.

He knew, wrote Miriam, that she had Power, but that it flowed in different channels from that of her peers and so they didn't understand her. He, while not presuming to understand her, had been working with the energy she was attuned to for quite some time. He had a group. Would she care to come to one of their meetings?

Of course she would—who wouldn't, with a sell like that? And Miriam, bless her heart, had written the directions he gave her into her magical notebook.

I copied them—it involved taking the F train to Queens and a bunch of other things. She hadn't written the address, just something on the order of "third building on the left, seventh floor, ring bell." But I could find the place if I had to. If I wanted to. If I was stupid.

The next couple of pages were lists of god-names, herbs, the Cyrillic alphabet copied out with its English equivalents next to it. Do you know that the Cyrillic alphabet has thirty-three letters, of which three are double consonants? I thought you didn't. Apparently her first meeting with the group had gone well, and Miriam was working on learning all the in-group trivia of yet another spiritual pathway.

Then there was a shopping list of sorts. It looked like Miriam was going to a ritual and had a list of things to bring. Probably a dedication. Innocent enough. Most groups have them—they give the seeker something to hold on to emotionally while s/he's being trained for initiation. Moon in Pisces; we were in April now.

One of the items on the list was a good recent photo. I thought of the likeness in the front of the "prayer book." Somebody had taken Miriam's measure in more ways than one.

Another was an *athame.* Or any double-edged knife. Miriam would have taken them the best she had. Her Ironshadow blade.

So where was it now?

The next several pages were rituals, probably copied out from typed Xeroxes they'd given her once they decided she was trustable. It was pretty standard stuff, based heavily on the

Gardnerian model with a lot of Crowley thrown in, and garnished with heavy pseudo-Russian Old Gods.

There was certainly a pre-Christian religion in Russia—in fact several of them, since the now-defunct Union of Soviet Socialist Republics (which everybody calls Russia and which isn't) covered one-quarter of the Earth's land mass. This religion was probably nasty, brutish, and shamanic, as so many of the subsistence-level cold-climate Paganisms are.

But we don't *know*. And probably never will. And anything calling itself a reconstruction is going to be nine-tenths fantasy and one-tenth plagiarism. Miriam's group's stuff was just Russian-flavored pseudo-Gardnerianism with a ritual magic chaser. Miriam probably would have moved on from this, too.

The rest of the pages were blank, I thought, but I flipped through to be sure. In the last few pages toward the end I found that Miriam had taken up her diarizing again.

Unlike her usual flowing hand these were written tiny and crabbed, as if Miriam didn't want to see them herself. None of them was dated, but after a few minutes I realized the earliest one was the last—which meant you had to start at the end and work backwards—and after that it was fairly easy.

But oh, what they said. My heart hurt for Miriam, and at the same time I was so mad at her that if she'd been here right now I would have strangled her. How could anyone be that stupid? I asked myself. How could she stay when they did that to her?

The people at the battered women's shelters ask that every day. And the ones in Children's Services. And the cops. How could he-she-they-it let anyone do that?

Miriam (I guessed) was dedicated into the Queens coven. The next thing they asked for was her blood and bone. I don't know where she got the bone. Baby teeth probably, if she'd saved any of hers. The blood had been drawn at a covenmeet. The site had become infected. She'd started having nightmares.

Put it on paper and it sounds laughable—the "Saturday Night Live" version of *Rosemary's Baby*. But the fear came through even in the cryptic notes that were the only thing Miriam allowed herself to write.

That, and her justifications for what the coven did. How she was stupid to make a fuss. Stupid to be afraid.

They asked for more and more, but what they asked for didn't make it onto paper—only Miriam's anger with how afraid they made her, her triumph each time she managed to do something against all her better instincts. Her statements about how her fear was the last barrier between her and Power. How it would pass. Soon.

Oh please Goddess soon she wrote. And started to cross it out. And didn't.

How could she let them do that to her?

Easy.

She forgot she was a grown-up.

Our childhood is spent doing things against our will. Against our instincts, our desires, our judgment (such as it is) we're compelled to do things we don't want to do. Eat our vegetables. Wash. Go to school. And usually we look back on those things later and realize they were the right things to do at the time.

Childhood is about trust. And somewhere in most of us the trusting child lives on. And sometimes, years later, it can be lured into horror, step by step, by the voice that says: *Just do it. I know what's best. You need to do this. It's best for you.*

The icons of Manson and Jonestown are never far from us, and sometimes adulthood is the easiest thing to give away when people ask us to give them things. Some people thrust their adulthood into any hands even halfway willing to take it. I didn't know where to assign the blame. I only knew my chest hurt.

I tucked my extended museum collection of Miriam's life in a safe place and hit the streets, burying anger in motion. I spent the rest of the day making the rounds—Aphrodisia, Weiser's, The Snake—and telling people about Miriam's death and Changing's open circle.

I should have stopped in at the Revel, too, but then I would have had to admit to Carrie that I'd known about Miriam's being dead when I'd been there Friday and hadn't told her.

Actually, social cowardice can be a rewarding, self-affirming life path.

Chores done and social outrage put away, I picked up a six-pack of Tsingtao I couldn't really afford and headed home to share it with the little Goddess. Work in the morning. So much for a wild weekend in the earthly paradise.

But if the Khazar coven was so goddamn medieval in its arts and graces, where *was* Miriam's *athame?*

Raymond was pleased with the work I'd done on the poetry spreads—which was nice, but what really matters is what the client thinks. Most of them have an annoying ability to expect the impossible and see what isn't there.

As a reward for my yeoman service, Ray gave me a mammoth job that'd just come in from Flatiron Press—one of the last great independent New York publishers, down on 23rd Street. It really was a reward, even though it looked like a bitch of a job, because it meant I'd have no trouble working enough hours to pay my rent for the foreseeable future.

I carted it back to my table and looked it over. It was unusual for us to get a job from Flatiron. Flatiron still does most of their stuff in-house, unless they get something like this. My life's partner for about the next three months: weight about ten pounds, all found. It was a huge, messy manuscript—and stats, and boards— that seemed to be about "how to build your own Victorian house from granite rocks." It had twelve million pictures and drawings that all had to fall on the same spread as their call-outs, no exception.

A call-out is book-design jargon for the reference in the text. When the text says: "The Adam-style fireplace, with ornamental liripipe and ruched gonfanons, represents—" the picture or drawing it cites has to be on the same spread— which is design jargon for any two facing pages. Even-numbered pages are always on the left side of a spread, because page one always starts on the right and has a blank facing page.

It didn't take me long to learn that. Anyone could. But then, nobody wants my job.

So I spread it out and settled in to a nice, peaceful, noncreative fug, which should carry me safely into the fall, when there are more interesting things to think about than work. At lunch I deposited Miriam's last paycheck, emptied her account as far as the ATM would let me, bought a money order, and dropped my package for Shelbyville off at the UPS.

On Tuesday Rachel Seabrook called, to tell me the UPS package containing Miriam's personal effects had gotten there and to tell me what the police had said when they called. There would be an autopsy of Miriam's body, as in all cases of accidental death. It was a routine procedure. On the other hand, Rachel couldn't expect to see results, death certificate, or body until the end of August.

"What am I going to do? I can't just pretend she's still alive!"

I recommended a lawyer and a memorial service. I told Rachel there would be a memorial service here on Friday. I told her she could almost certainly get Miriam cremated and scattered without having to fly her home. I got off the phone before I promised to arrange any of these things.

Maybe it wasn't going to be such a quiet week after all.

Thursday, June 21, was the summer solstice—the longest day of the year. It was also the last day before the dark moon, which probably explained my mood. It's a little-known fact that human craziness shows a measurable upswing on the dark, or new, moon as well as on the full, but I didn't feel crazy. I just felt depressed. It was a real effort to leave Houston Graphics right at five and catch the Uptown train for Bellflower's.

Belle lives mostly by herself in a rambling apartment in Washington Heights and does not believe in spending money on furniture. The elevator was broken again, so I walked up the five flights of stairs and leaned on the bell. This week it was wired up to a recording of a kazoo playing *Ode to Joy.*

"We ordered Indian take-away," Dorje said, once I finished hugging Belle hello. "You want to go in on it?"

"Sure," I said.

I looked around the living room, counting heads. Since this was a weekday, and Changing has frequently been accused of being a yuppie coven (meaning most of us have nine-to-five jobs that prefer we show up for them), anybody who couldn't afford a late night was doing private ritual at home to mark Longest Day and would gather here tomorrow for Miriam's Crossing.

Counting Belle and me we were five so far

(Changing is an actual thirteen-member coven, when we all show up). The Cat was here, of course—she's a student who lives, none too happily, with her parents and appreciates any chance to get away from them. Sundance has a car and a night job out on the Island Thursday through Monday, and Dorje lives two blocks away, so they were here, and Glitter and Beaner might make it later, dea volente.

These are their Craft names—the names they took when they decided to become Witches. Their "real" names are none of your business— or mine, although I know most of them. Their Craft names *are* them, and a lot more vivid than John, James, Jane, or Heather.

Glitter is Glitter because she wears purple lamé to work. She's an NYC probation officer, which means Civil Service, vested with a pension, and just *try* to fire her for violation of dress code. She gets a lot more fun out of life than she would if she worked somewhere they approved of her. She also carries the world's only—thank god—purple-rhinestone-hilted *athame.*

The Cat looks like one—a brown tabby, say, with all those fingerprint-swirls of black through her fur. It's caused by interlocking dye jobs that make her the sole support of Lady Clairol. The Cat goes to City College. She's been going for years. Her hobby is Making Things Work—the kazoo doorbell was her creation. She's been trying to get me to let her record a tape for my answering machine, but I've heard the one she did for Dorje.

Sundance's name comes from a long, elabo-

rate, and mostly forgotten joke about mad dogs
and Englishmen. You'd say he was painfully
normal—except for the fact that his wife left him
and took the kids when he went into the broom
closet. Beaner is from Brahmin stock—the pahk
ya cah in Hahvahd Yahd kind. Gay as a cavalier
and a tenor for the Light Opera of Manhattan.
His father's somebody in the foreign service and
according to Beaner can't make up his mind
which is worse: a Pooh-Bah who's a Witch or A
Son Of His singing on the public stage.

The kazoo played *Ode to Joy* again. Dorje got
the door this time—Glitter and the food arrived
together. I flopped down on Belle's emotional
rescue couch and stretched out.

And try as I might, I couldn't stop thinking
about that other coven. Miriam's coven, the one
she'd tithed to in blood and bone and tears, the
coven that seemed set up to be a mockery of
everything I knew the Craft to be.

Survivor's guilt, they call it.

I got back to my apartment late—or early, depending on your point of view. The ritual had
gone well, and I'd talked out some of what I felt
about Miriam. We all agreed that it was Too Bad
she'd gotten involved with rough trade, but that
it was Not My Fault, no matter what I'd bought
her. I received a stern lecture on borrowing trouble—"Why bother?" said Dorje. "You get so
much of it free."—or not borrowing trouble, as
the case might be. Plans for the open circle tomorrow night were set. The Cat promised to put
it on the NYC Pagan BBS—that's computer bul-

letin board, for those of us not quite technoliterate.

When I got in I found my answering machine light was flashing with what turned out to be half a dozen disconnects. This is an annoying but unavoidable complication of having one of the damn things, and I didn't want to listen to it have seizures all night. I turned it off and the phone bell down low, and went to bed.

A long time later I woke up from a vague unpleasant dream of a dentist doing root-canal work to a muted rhythmic bleating. It was still dark outside. After about a dozen rings I identified the sound as my phone.

After about six more rings I realized it wasn't going to stop, and that somebody must want to reach me pretty badly. My bedside clock said 3:45 A.M. I groped over to the phone.

"Hello?"

"Miriam doesn't need your help. Call off the ritual, Witch-bitch, or somebody's going to put your eyes out."

He hung up and I hit the light switch and sat there in a small pool of halogen wishing I still smoked. Anything. Useless adrenaline made the inside of my mouth metallic. I replayed the call in my mind.

Hate. Enough of it to up my heart rate. And not the same voice that had called Miriam's apartment and been so stunned when someone answered.

I got up and walked, to keep my mind from feeding its memory of the call until it tried to open up a link between me and my caller. I put on the tea-water. I opened a beer. I wrote down the date and time and text of the phone call and drank my beer and my tea and watched the clock tick over numerals to 4:38 A.M.

The caller was the same one responsible for all those hang-ups. I was morally certain of this on the basis of no evidence. He wanted me to call off the memorial service for Miriam, as if I could. And he didn't like me or my eyes, which was just too bad for him.

But there was one little thing that was just too bad for me, and it kept me awake until six A.M. when I could reasonably go into the studio early.

He knew who I was, he knew I was a Witch, and he'd called me at home.

But my number's unlisted.

Friday the 22nd had started out just dandy and got better. I was in the studio about seven A.M. Around ten the phone rang.

"It's for you!" Ray yelled in my direction. He held the phone as if he intended to fling it to the floor. No personal calls on studio time allowed, so anybody calling me had to be stupid or the bearer of bad news.

I went over and picked up the phone.

"May I help you?"

"Bast?" Lace again. My stomach tied itself into knots.

"Uh, Lace, is this an emergency?" Oh please, Goddess, let it not be.

Lace took a deep breath. "There's been somebody in Miriam's apartment, Bast. I think you better see."

So in the end I had to thank my midnight caller for allowing me to put in all those early-morning hours at Houston Graphics so I could take a nice long lunch hour. I spent the subway ride north practicing my paranoia.

Lace has my home number. So do about a dozen other people who know me as Bast-the-Witch. Houston Graphics has it, for emergencies, whatever a design studio emergency might be, written right next to the name they use on my paychecks.

It's on the business cards identifying it as the number for High Tor Graphics, which is the name under which I do my freelance work. None of those clients know me as Bast. In point of cold hard fact, there's nothing anywhere to connect High Tor Graphics with Bast.

I'd be willing to bet my last pentacle that nobody I knew in the Craft would hand over my number to any stranger asking for Bast's phone number, and my midnight caller was as strange as they come.

So where had he gotten it? And what possible objection could he have to an entirely benign Neopagan funeral ritual for Miriam Seabrook?

And exactly how up close and personal did he intend to get?

Lace was standing in the doorway to Miriam's apartment when I got there.

"Did you lock the goddamn door?" she demanded as soon as she saw me.

Lace had worked through her fear very nicely, thank you, and was now on her way to furious.

"No, I'm the village idiot. Of course I locked it."

"The hell you did." It came out "hail," from somewhere south of what author Florence King calls the "Smith & Wesson Line." "You just take a looky here."

She backed up and let me in. I looked around the living room, saw what I didn't expect to see, and sat down on the couch. Fast.

Miriam's apartment had been thoroughly tossed. Books thrown all over the floor, records out of their jackets, tapes unwound, stomped, and thrown about. Pillows slashed. Curtains pulled down. All the pieces of Miriam's altar swept off the bookcase top and smashed. I was glad I'd taken the little Goddess home with me.

But Miriam's real expensive sound system, her one brand-new and high-ticket purchase, was still sitting right where I'd left it.

"You left the goddamn door open, Bast!" Lace said again.

I'd locked it, but when she's like this Lace punches people who contradict her.

"Was the door locked when you got here?" I asked.

"Sure it was. I— Oh." Lace looked around the room and back at me. "It was locked," she said. Anger drained out of her like water down the bathtub drain, leaving someone I could talk to.

"And we had the only keys. Right?"

Lace wasn't sure. The building super, I knew, had one, and Miriam might have given out others. But I couldn't think of anyone who wouldn't just have taken things away.

"Okay," I said. "Let's look around." Lace wandered into the living room, scuffing through the wreckage. I went into the kitchen.

True, the place was a mess, but not as bad as if it had been tossed by thrill-burglars (who locked up after themselves?). For instance, the plates weren't broken—although everything had been taken out of the cupboards and the refrigerator door had been left open. Somebody had been looking for something.

The bedroom was the worst.

The mattress was off the box spring. Both the bedside lamps were smashed—which was pure temper. All the drawers were torn out of the dresser. The closet had been emptied. The two footlockers that I'd gone through so carefully on Saturday were tipped up on end, their contents flung around the room.

"I thought I better come up and look at it today, so we could get the stuff out by the end of the month." Lace came in behind me and was standing looking around, as much stricken as angry. "It was *locked*."

Somebody had indeed been looking for something.

"Lace, whatever happened to Miriam's *athame*? Her ritual knife?" I added, just in case Lace was being too Dianic this week to remember what they were called.

Lace took another step into the room. Something beneath the papers went crunch under her boots. She bent down and picked up part of a porcelain plate. It had brown smudges where Miriam used to burn cone incense on it.

"They took it."

It took me a minute to realize this was a question.

"No. I went through everything when I was here. I found the rest of her tools, but I didn't find her knife. Did she leave it with you?" It was a stupid question, but sometimes lovers do stupid things.

Lace shrugged irritably. "Forged iron's patriarchal, anyway."

Maybe it is, but we live in a sexually dimorphic universe and play by the House rules. "Sure, but have you seen her knife?" And I'd rather have my will symbolized by a dagger than a shrub.

"No, I haven't seen her goddamn *altecocker* knife! And what I want to know is, who came in here and tore this place up?"

"And what were they looking for?" I added.

Lace turned around, mad again and reminding me uncomfortably of a buffalo about to charge. One of the nasty African ones. Lace is frequently silly, and ludicrous, and lives in her own private Idaho, but she is not stupid. As science fiction's patron saint John W. Campbell was so fond of saying: "thinks as well as a man but not like one."

"What *were* they looking for, Bast?" Lace said dangerously.

"I don't know." But I did. The Khazar book. Miriam's diaries. Her necklace.

"And who are they?" Lace added.

"I'm not sure," I said.

Lace's face got that flat intent look it does just before she brains some other dyke with a full beer bottle.

"I'm *not*," I insisted. "I'm trying to find out— you remember I asked you who she was with when she died?"

Inflection is all. I wasn't asking Lace who'd been at the apartment, nor yet who Miriam had been romantically involved with. "Who are you with?" in the Community has just one meaning: What coven are you in?

"You think those *Baklava* people came here and did this? *Pagans* wouldn't do this!"

Oh, my people. For some of us it is still Woodstock time, with the Neopagan Community replacing the counterculture. And we are all of one ethos, and would never prey upon one another.

Even among hippies this idea lasted about fifteen minutes, but Lace would rather believe this hadn't happened at all than that it had been done by a fellow Goddess-worshiper.

"It has to have been somebody else. And I'm going to find them. And when I do . . ." Lace promised.

Any Gardnerian knows better. The infighting that's gone on in our branch of the Craft since the sainted Gerald Gardner died makes us look like a bunch of Protestants.

"Sure," I said for Lace's benefit. "But you know, if she was working with them, maybe her group'd know who it could be. And when I find out for sure, I'll tell you."

Lace made a noise like a downshifting truck.

"I promise," I said hastily. "Lace, there isn't any more we can do. We aren't even supposed to be in here. What do you want to do—call the police?"

It took me two hours to settle Lace down and stop her going door-to-door with a baseball bat. By then she'd called some of her friends to come over and help with the cleaning and scavenging, and Miriam's place was full of well-adjusted women with large muscles.

I went back to the studio. I had no trouble getting sympathy over my story of a friend whose apartment had been tossed. It's as common as having your apartment searched by the KGB used to be. In the old days. In Russia.

Russia. Khazar Trad. And a bunch of people starting to look a lot more organized, motivated, and twisted than any Pagans I'd ever seen outside of bad fiction.

A bunch of people who were looking for *me*.

4

By seven o'clock Friday night I was a nervous wreck and desperately in need of at least five of the six beers I'd refused to let myself have. For one, it isn't a good idea to ride the subway while impaired because to survive in Fun City requires constant alertness. For the other, it's a damn poor idea to walk into a circle under any influence other than magic. It's disrespectful to the Gods, and it could leave you with your psyche in a mangle.

How mangled had Miriam's psyche gotten? I shoved the thought aside. No matter what had happened, the Community was going to do right by her tonight.

Bellflower's place was jammed. Sundance took one look at me and handed me the beer he'd just opened.

"You could use it," he said. He had to raise his voice to be heard over the dull roar of three dozen people yammering at once.

"Thanks," I yelled back. I made the beer go

away and shook my head when he offered me a refill. Somebody started playing with Belle's sound system and an old Leigh Ann Hussey tape added "The Goddess Done Left Me" to the general noise level.

"I'm sorry about Miriam," Sundance said.

"People die," I snapped back, sharper than I'd intended. "Yeah, well, it's harder on Lace," I emended.

"I think I saw her here," Sundance said, and about then Glitter and The Cat saw me and carried me off.

"I remember Miriam. She was a good person. She always took time to help you out."

The speaker was a man, someone I didn't know. Since this was an open circle we were meeting in street clothes. He had on a tie-dyed T-shirt silk-screened with roses and skulls. He passed the talking-stick to the woman on his right.

"I remember Sunshrike. One time we invited another coven for Sabbat, and Sunshrike made twelve dozen oatmeal raisin cookies. She cleaned up after, too."

There were about forty people jammed into Belle's living room, making a wobbly oval circle-by-courtesy that filled the living room, the foyer, and wandered into the kitchen. Belle had cast the circle in her best ecumenical style and used the Neopagan Crossing ritual that almost everyone would know, the one that starts: "We are here to say farewell to a friend who must travel far." Then she started the talking-stick around. When it got to you, you said good-bye.

I'd put myself opposite the altar. The stick had a ways to go before it reached me. I wondered what I'd say.

I also wondered if any of the people here had called me up real early this morning. Or had a key to Miriam's apartment.

But I still couldn't figure out a *reason*. It's true that we're none of us angels, and a lot of people hiding behind some fancy Neopagan or New Age handle are as thoroughly bad-hat as they come. But they're almost always mundanes looking for the money to be made off gulling the marks—not believers themselves.

Maybe the Neopagans learned from the mistakes of the previous winners in the World Religion Sweepstakes. Maybe a collection of religious practices exalting *laissez-faire* and everybody finding his own path to divinity just can't spark the moral indignation needed for a pogrom. My personal favorite belief is that we're just too disorganized.

But the cold fact is that I've *never* heard of a real case of intramural lawlessness in the Craft or the Community on purely doctrinal grounds. Name-calling and tiffs, yes. Head-tripping like what Miriam had recorded, yes. But never any real-for-true Pagan-to-Pagan police blotter stuff.

And while my hate call early this morning could be business as usual in the peace-love-and–rock'n'roll Pagan Community, the person-or-people who'd ransacked Miriam's apartment and left behind everything of resale value wasn't.

But my conviction that all the weirdness that had happened was directly related to Miriam's last religious affiliation barely convinced even me, and I'd known all these people intimately for years. As an actual accusation to bring in the mundane courts, it was hopeless.

The person on my right bumped me and handed me the talking-stick.

"I knew Miriam Seabrook. She was a friend. I hope she finds what she's looking for. Good-bye, Sunshrike." I passed the stick to the left.

Everybody hung around after the circle was over. A lot of people had brought cookies or chips or soda and I'd chipped in $5.00 to the Changing general fund for more. The gathering wasn't solemn like a mundane funeral—more like a wake is supposed to be, I'd guess. Most people here hadn't known Miriam very well, and most of them were still young and flaky enough to think that their death would never come.

If the Craft has any failings at all as a religion, it's that it doesn't really do a very good job of taking people through the absolute gut-crunching worst that Life can do. The Lady's mercy was a consolation to me, but I'd be damned hesitant about offering the joys of the Summerland to a mother whose child had just been killed by a drunk driver. People tend to forget that the Craft is the newest religion, as well as the oldest. Maybe it's just that the human race has gotten arrogant enough that the phrase "It's God's will, it's for the best," isn't good enough anymore. Maybe it's never been good enough and we're just admitting it now.

Or maybe the Lady shows Her true face now, as ever, only to those who can manage their lives without a convenient god to blame.

I don't know. Ask me in fifty years when the Craft starts building churches.

Lace came over to me with Tollah; Carrie must be minding the Revel. Lace's eyes were red and she hugged me, and we ended up hanging out in a back bedroom at Belle's with a couple other of Miriam's particular friends for a few hours telling each other the ten stupidest things Miriam had ever done.

"There was this one time—you've got to hear this, Lace; I bet she never told you," a woman named Andre was saying, "when me and Miriam and a bunch of that coven from Fort Lee went out to one of the old Pan-Pagan Festivals in Indiana. And for the main circle they had these big thirty-gallon water-cooler jugs up on top of pillars and they'd dumped this chemical in them to make them glow. So the next time I turn around she's walking up to one to get a drink out of it, right?—you know the stuff's poisonous?—and when I stopped her she said she thought it was just water and they were glowing because of the power we raised in circle!"

"Magic Power of Witchcraft," several of us said in ragged chorus. It's one of those old Community jokes: There's a difference in believing in the power of the Lady and thinking you're Samantha of "Bewitched."

Had Miriam ever found it out?

The Crossing ritual had settled my mind, despite my usual misgivings about the Craft as a full-service religion. Miriam was now beyond any earthly hele or ill, and we had done what we could to speed her safe on her way. Having done that, I had the emotional distance to sort things out in my mind.

Unfortunately, I didn't like what I found.

Item: Last Friday, the day she died, Miriam called me. Upset. Very upset. She had to see me. I knew Miriam frequently but not intimately. Since then I'd had cause to wonder how well Miriam thought she knew *me*.

Item: Some time after her call Miriam Seabrook, age thirty-two, lay down and died. Literally.

Item: From all the written evidence, Miriam was into a pretty bad-hat form of Neopaganism. I thought about the phone call I'd intercepted at her apartment and decided it didn't prove anything at all.

Item: In the wee small hours of this very Friday morning, somebody phoned me up to try to stop tonight's ritual and to tell me with menaces that "Miriam didn't need my help." So far, this was my only grounds for thinking that any of this had to do with Miriam's new religion.

Item: Somewhere between last Saturday and this afternoon, somebody entered Miriam's apartment with a key. They turned the place inside out looking for something, but didn't take anything of mundane value that they found. Oh, yes—and they locked up when they left.

Item: Miriam's *athame* was missing—at least, it hadn't been there when *I* searched the place.

These were all terrific facts. It was just too bad they didn't add up to much.

Miriam had been scared before she died. True, her coven had probably been head-tripping her, but did I trust Miriam to be scared only for a good reason? No. Did I see any connection between Miriam's phone call and her death? No.

Did I want to find out more about the Khazar Trad and whether it was them Miriam was scared of?

You figure it out.

I was one of the last people to leave Belle's. It was about three in the morning and we were down to coven and one or two hangers-on—the kind of people who leave any party about ten minutes after the host has gone to bed. Lace had left a couple hours ago, probably to cruise some of the dyke bars in the East Village and find something to stuff in the big empty of never being able to share a joke with Miriam again.

Belle wanted me to stay the night, but Beaner and The Cat already were—and besides, there's something about wandering the city at this hour. It's one of life's riskier pleasures, but if you haven't got a taste for risky pleasures, why live here?

I hit the street. It was empty. The air had that peculiar softness it acquires, regardless of the season, after three o'clock in the morning. The sky would be showing light by the time I got home, probably, and the predawn breeze was already up.

Spanish Harlem moves farther north and west every year; most of the shops down on Dyckman are bilingual. But even they had given up and gone to sleep. It was just me, and the long wall of High Bridge Park on my right. My boots made sharp quiet sounds on sidewalk the color of old pewter.

There is beauty in the city's artificial stone. But there's a lot more harm. To the Environment, people call it, as if it's nothing to do with them. As if, if the Environment were all gone, there would still be someplace to live.

Illiteracy has a lot to answer for. Environment is just a long word for where-you-are.

I heard footsteps on the street behind me. Probably somebody leaving Belle's after me, wanting to catch up. I slowed down and made the automatic, ever-so-subtle, look-over-the-shoulder gesture.

Nobody. So I picked it up again, heading down the hill.

Footsteps. And now that they'd stopped and hid once I was very interested in them, so I stopped dead and looked outright, because maiden modesty kills more New Yorkers every year than AIDS.

Nobody.

Or was that a flutter of movement from some-body ducking into something just out of my line of sight?

Why find out for sure?

So I crossed the street and didn't hear any more footsteps.

The Dyckman/200th Street Station is the next-to-last stop on the A line. It is down one of those bad old twisty subway stops, and no matter how many "Off-Hour Waiting Area" signs the MTA puts up, nobody is going to wait in them for fear of missing their train. Waiting in them wouldn't make you any safer, anyway.

The station has a long flight down, then a landing with a right angle to another half flight of stairs. Then you're down at token-booth level (closed, at this hour). From the bottom of the stairs you can't see the top.

The platform is on the same level as the booth, cut off from it by a combination of tile walls and a big iron fence with a set of old-fash-ioned wooden turnstiles. You can't see the whole platform from the token booth area, which can be unnerving.

The station extends the width of Broadway and there are accesses from both sides. You can walk across Broadway from below if you're of a mind to, and go up the stairs at the other end, or you can pay your fare, go through the turnstiles, and have your choice of uptown and downtown trains.

I'd just reached the right-turn landing and

was starting down into the station when I heard footsteps behind me, skipping down the stairs. I did one of the basic Directed Imaging exercises real fast—"Visualize a cloudbank. Now wrap it around you so that you're wearing a cloak of mist. Nothing can reach you through this cloak"—and hurried out onto the platform. If the footsteps were following me I wasn't sure I could get across the station and up the other stairs before they saw me—and even if I did it wouldn't be a lot of help.

For once I beat the fare—I didn't want the person following to hear the turnstile go clunk. I got out of line-of-sight and stood in the corner by the pass-under to the uptown trains wearing my cloudbank and pretending I was uninteresting so hard my teeth hurt. I felt the wind on my face that meant a train was moving in the tunnel, and concentrated on making it come here fast.

I heard the footsteps outside the token booth. I couldn't be seen except from the platform itself—I wondered if he was a scofflaw, too, or would think it worth paying a dollar-plus to make sure I wasn't here.

The footsteps crossed the area in front of the token booth, then started up the steps on the other side.

The train pulled into the station. I lunged into it before the doors finished opening and crouched low between the seats pretending I wasn't there. If my shadow got on the train at all he could hopscotch cars at the next station and find me.

The doors closed and the train began to move. I saw someone run down the steps to the platform, but it could have been anyone.

Anyone at all.

So much for Friday.

The trouble was that all of this could be coincidence, or my nerves (which I'd used to think were good), or something real—either sacred or mundane.

And I had no way of finding out which, you should pardon the expression.

In fiction it's different. The detective goes around asking questions, stirring everyone up—and he gets answers. Even Kinsey Millhone gets answers.

If I tried that, everyone including my best friends would shut up like a clam.

We've lived with secrecy for too long. In 1963 when the Craft came over from England and the only kind of Witch there was, was Gardnerian, we hid. Nineteen sixty-three was before the Summer of Love. People advocating love and peace and trust were slightly to the left of UFO cultists on the Cultural Weirdness Scale. We learned to be secret to keep from losing our jobs and our kids and our credit ratings.

After the Glorious October of '79, when Margot Adler published *Drawing Down the Moon* and Starhawk published *The Spiral Dance* and Wicca and Neopaganism became boring instead of threatening, the habit of secrecy remained—even though by now the only ones asking questions were our own.

Oh, some secrets should be kept, and some should be revealed at the right time, but the simple fact is that keeping secrets and saying "I Can't Tell You" is *fun* for those of us who are full-grown in body only, and they have no intention of giving it up. The only way to get answers is to convince your listener you already know them.

The way to find out exactly how Miriam Seabrook died wasn't by asking questions.

Saturday. Miriam's directions would have been easier to follow if she hadn't left out every other one. Fortunately, I figured out from the street names that I was going to Queens, or I never would have known to take the uptown train.

I wasn't followed, this time.

I had no idea if I was going to the Khazar covenstead, or if I could even find it from Miriam's directions or recognize it when I had. And even if I could do all those things, what was I going to do then?

I replayed Miriam's last phone message in my mind. Whatever its cause, her fear was genuine.

And she'd called *me*. Why?

Think about it. She had a lover and she had a coven. If the problem was in the Real World, she'd have called Lace, not me, as Lace, believe it or not, is very good at dealing with other people's problems. If her problem was magical-with-a-*K*, she'd have called someone in her coven, right?

The only reason I could think of for her to call me was if the problem *was* her coven. Which brought me back to Square One, and, as it might be, Miriam's deathbed request.

Help her. And if she was dead, find out why.

Most of the "subway" lines in Queens are elevated, and any time I go there it gives me the feeling I've wandered through a spacewarp into Chicago—rows and rows of tenements built before World War II interspersed with the occasional McDonald's sign.

I counted stops until I reached the right one and got off, looking for Miriam's landmarks. It was dark under the tracks, and Manhattan felt about a million miles away. I located the bridal salon and the taverna and started walking.

Why was I doing this? I wasn't the Occult Police. Even if Miriam's covenleader was the original bad hat there was nothing I could do. I couldn't prove it to the mundane authorities, and nobody *ever* gets thrown out of the Craft. Not even Geordie Angel, who runs that fraud mail-order Christian Wicca course from a post-office box in Idaho and who, at the last Neopagan event he attended, slugged a friend of mine in the face. In front of a dozen witnesses, and of course no one even thought to charge him with assault.

Nobody cares. This is the essential meaning of entropy. And if nobody cared, then what I was doing was pointless, wasn't it?

Or was I just cruising to become a legend in my own mind, like all those well-known subway vigilantes?

I turned down a street that had a Gulf station on the right and a deli on the left and a laundromat at the end—according to Miriam's directions, the place she'd gone was on the right side of the street.

No restaurants. That meant she'd been invited into a private home, which is a little unusual on a first meeting.

It's unusual because there are a lot of kinks out there. I'd told Miriam and told her, and in the end I guessed it hadn't helped at all.

Miriam hadn't written the building number or the street name down, of course—the directions said something about "third door, seventh floor." Third door—or building—was the only one on the street that looked as if it could have that many floors. I went into the lobby.

The names on the buzzers for the seventh floor were either missing or seemed to date from when the building was new. No clue there as to which door Miriam had disappeared behind, but all the same I wanted to get out of there.

It was June and I'd never been here before, but I had a sudden flash of how the street would look in winter—cold and dead and sterile. Or worse, how it would look once everyone was gone, and the houses were all burnt-out grafitti-covered shells.

I did not run all the way back to the subway stop. I did *not*.

While I was waiting for the subway back to normalcy I wrote down the address I'd just been to. I felt creepy, as if I'd just burgled a funeral home or wandered into one of those strange rites only found in Thomas Tryon novels. I needed a good dose of Earth-plane reality, and I knew just where to get it.

Chanters Revel is decorous and politically correct. It is a credit to the fistful of Dianic, Feminist, and Goddess-oriented traditions it serves. Aphrodisia lets questions of religion pass it by—it's an herb store, period, and has no affiliations to shake a stick at. Weiser's, East-West Books, and Star Magic are all massively disinterested in what their clientele is into.

The Serpent's Truth is wildly partisan and unashamedly trashy.

They say it's in the Village, and they lie—as Edna St. Vincent Millay once similarly said in connection with Vassar and the Hudson River. The Official New York Northern Cutoff Point for Greenwich Village is Eighth Street (except in the minds of real estate salesmen), and The Snake is almost a dozen blocks north of that, up where the real estate's cheap—or was, back when anything in New York was cheap.

The Snake shares its street with the back of a parking garage, an S&M bar, a commercial photofinishing lab, a sleazy Greek coffee shop, and a store whose plate-glass window says "Novelties"—and lies. You can recognize The Snake by its Beyond Tacky neon sign. To be fair, the sign was there before The Snake was, and is almost certainly the reason for the store's name.

In the long decades of its career, the sign has lost all of the neon tubing that went to make up whatever name the previous business had. All that's left now is a neon picture of a walking stick with a bright green snake wrapped around it. When the sign's lit, the snake coils up and down the stick and flicks its tongue in and out. It fits, somehow.

Today the front window contained a crystal ball on a light-up stand, a selection of grimoires and magic wands, some ritual swords (stamped out of pot metal and liable to bend), and a dressmaker's dummy with a full set of Genuine Wizard's Robes on it, including a long pointy hat with silver stars that I coveted unreasonably. The store has double narrow doors, meant to both be open, but as usual only one was, and the six-foot-high Day-Glo Technicolor Mighty Wurlitzer jukebox containing every record Elvis ever made blocked the other half. Once you made it past that obstacle you were confronted by an eight-foot-high plaster statue of the Goat of Mendes and a jewelry case full of pentacles, bat earrings, and pendants made out of glass eyes. Some of them had made their way into my wardrobe in days gone by. The whole shop was Tourist City.

The Snake is not, and never has been, good press for the Community. It gets dished a lot. Just about all you can say in its defense is that it's been around a long time (it opened sometime in the early sixties), it provides a highly visible intake port for people looking for the Craft or something like it, and it has done less harm to more people than televangelism.

It is also definitely a more interesting place to be than the Revel. I slid in past the jukebox. When I'm especially unlucky, I get to the shop when Tris has decided to play it—the thing has speakers that'd make Metallica blush with envy.

There was the usual haze of frankincense up near the ceiling, and the whole back wall was filled by the lighted glass cabinet Tris (the owner) had just put in dedicated to the gris-gris and floorwash crowd. Between the floorwashes and the jewelry case were the books: Wicca on the right, Magick on the left, Rosicrucianism and what-have-you down the middle. There were also herbs, thunderstones, herbal smudges, do-it-yourself voodoo-doll kits, candleholders in the shape of gargoyles, wishing mirrors, scrying glasses, stained-glass pentacles, salt-and-water bowls, and polyester acetate wizard robes like the one in the window.

To say the stock is overcrowded is an understatement. The place is a retail designer's nightmare. If Tris (it's short for Trismegistus, actually) ever cleans this place he'll find the Lost Ark of the Covenant in the storeroom. Guaranteed.

Julian was at his usual post, behind the cash register. The checkout is on a built-up platform that raises it about eighteen inches off the floor. Julian resembled a scrivener in a Herman Melville story.

When the jukebox is running I deduct ten points from my Karma Batting Average. When Julian's behind the desk it's a plus ten. It was with a moderate amount of difficulty that I reined in my libido. Ah, if only . . .

Not that Julian's to everybody's taste: Unless your fancy runs to pale, tubercular intellectuals with lank black hair you won't have much use for him. Julian is, among other things, a Ceremonial Magician. I've heard it said that he's the only person ever to have actually done the entire Abra-Melin Ritual, which takes a year to perform and requires you to own your own lakeside cottage.

His sexual preferences, if any, are a mystery to the entire Community, which is good as it keeps me (barely) from acting like an utter fool in his presence, further encouraged in this laudable aim only by his utter indifference to me except as a source of Visa receipts. It would be a lot more comfortable if I could reciprocate said indifference, but there's precious little hope of that. Maybe it's those silly little glasses.

"Hi, Julian, got a minute?" I asked. I wasn't being overfamiliar; he may have a last name, but I've never heard it. And on this occasion I had a perfectly legitimate reason for engaging him in a conversation unrelated to spending money.

Julian peered down at me and glare turned his glasses white. Sigh. He was, as usual, wearing a Roman collar (which he may be entitled to, for all I know), a secondhand hammertail coat, and those tiny oval clerk's glasses. I have always admired Julian's fashion statements. They make no concession to the twentieth century, which is why he makes such an admirable manager for The Snake.

"Oh hi, Bast," Julian said vaguely. "Your books are in."

This is Julian's standard greeting to me. When I tell him, as I do, that I haven't ordered any books, he either tries to convince me that I have (in an amnesiac moment) or that I would have if I'd heard of them.

This was a hands-down case of the second category.

The book he unearthed was a facsimile copy of John Dee's *Talismantic Intelligencer*, which is not, as you may think from the title, a small-town occult newspaper. I'd drooled over it when it came up in the Weiser's catalog a few years back but couldn't afford it. Limited edition, gold-stamped slipcase, bound-in ribbon bookmark, hand-sewn signatures, and guaranteed not to fit any bookcase I owned.

"They reprinted," Julian said. I pulled out my Visa.

"I'd kind of like your opinion on something." I stepped up onto the raised platform of the checkout cubbyhole while Julian rummaged around under his desk for the charge slips. "Ever seen anything like this?"

I dug the Khazar book out of my purse and waved it at him.

Julian came up—without the slips—and grabbed the book. I'd come to him not for slav-ish hormonal reasons but because Julian is that unpredictable—and rare—commodity, a scholar. The history of magic is his specialty.

"Nice work. Yours?" Julian flipped through it and came back to the icon.

"No. I got it from a friend. I was wondering about the Trad."

"Looks Slavic," Julian said. "Very ceremo-nial." He paged through it again and stopped to read. He could probably read the Russian too, damn him. "Sort of an ecological version of Rasputin," he said and handed it back to me.

"Rasputin—the guy who murdered the little princes in the tower?" I asked, just to be provoking.

Julian adjusted his little glasses and regarded me disapprovingly. "Grigory Efimovitch, popularly known as Rasputin, or 'The Dissolute,' magical healer and spiritual advisor to the court of the last Tsar of Russia—that's Nicholas the Second, if you're counting. He was thought to be able to cure the *Tsarevitch*'s hemophiliac attacks by prayer and the laying on of hands. His major contribution to religious thought is the doctrine of 'sinning in order for God to have something to forgive.'"

"God: That's Adonai Elohim, right?"

Julian actually smiled; the two years I'd spent studying Kabbalah weren't wasted. "But what *is* this?" I asked. "What's it *for?*"

"It's a prayer book," Julian repeated patiently. "A devotional—for raising magical power by prayer. You Witches don't go in much for that sort of thing."

"I've raised some power in my time, Julian," I pointed out. Wiccan and pseudo-Wiccan groups just don't go in for prayer as an end in itself.

"But then you used it yourself. This is obviously a . . . Think of it as a funnel. A link. The power is poured into the godform shown in the book—probably an artificial elemental of some sort—and then siphoned off later. At least it could be, if that was what they were doing," said Julian the ever-cautious.

Craft slang for people who siphon and store energy is "vampire."

"So it's not a Wiccan thing," I said, very casual. "My friend said it was a new Trad. Too bad; someone should do something with Russian Paganism." Why, I don't know—it's just one of those things a person says to fill up a gap in the conversation.

"You can't tell from this whether they're Witches or not. Polytheists, certainly, but most of this is rewarmed Golden Dawn, the usual mishmash; the only thing really original is the ecological nihilism. There's this guy in Queens doing a Russian Wicca coven. Very into secrecy. Very high church. Calls his group *Baba Yaga.* You could ask him about this—if you're interested, I could let him know."

Baba Yaga. Or, as Lace might hear it, *Baklava.*

Bingo.

"Do you know anything about them?"

Julian frowned. "No. Like I said, they're very secretive. I don't think they'll even talk to you unless you're vouched for. If this is theirs, that friend of yours might be able to get you in."

"And they're C.M.?" I prodded.

"If they are, nobody knows them." Which meant that Julian didn't know them, and Julian knew every serious practitioner of ritual magic on the Eastern seaboard.

The name *Baba Yaga* was tickling something in the back of my mind, and I wasn't sure what.

"Cindy might know," Julian added, trying to be helpful.

"Yeah," I said. "Thanks."

He bagged my book and I decided to take his advice. I went off to see if Cindy was home.

I should have remembered that Julian is never helpful.

5

L ife in the Community often resembles the peripateisis of the Edwardian novel. You go here, you visit, you go there, you visit. It isn't so much caused by the Community as by the City.

This is New York in June, which means intermittently hot, verging on beastly. Most of the people I know live in a tiny apartment or fraction thereof that either doesn't have an air conditioner or has one that the landlord won't let them run. Add to this the fact that anybody who *is* home isn't answering the phone for one of the following reasons:

A) It's hooked up to the fax/modem
B) He's too paranoid to answer it
C) There isn't one because his roommate stole it

and you have the reason why members of the Community spend their weekends wandering from deli to bookstore to apartment to coffee shop, hoping against hope that one of them will be air-conditioned.

Cindy is the first person who realized all of this, and, in a dazzling bid for popularity, bought a commercial air conditioner and stayed home.

Actually, that's only half the truth. Cindy has a typesetting and design service called Incendiary (her last name is Airey—at least it is now) that she runs out of the same loft she lives in. She specializes in catalogs—like Tree of Wisdom, The Snake's mail-order service, or Witchwife, the occult jewelers.

Cindy's street-level front door is one of those industrial-strength gray riveted things. Saturdays she keeps it propped open with a brick. Once you drag the door open you're confronted with a long narrow flight of stairs that goes up to Cindy's third-floor loft and no place else. There is no light bulb because the ceiling of the staircase—and the stairs are narrow—is about thirty feet away. I have always wondered how she got two thousand pounds of Computronic typesetter up them.

I trudged to the top of the stairs. On Saturdays the door at the top of the stairs is unlocked, too.

Cindy is about five foot two and looks like what God could have made out of me if She'd (1) had money and (2) meant me to go through life as a French maid in a bedroom farce. We both have black hair and blue eyes, but where Cindy looks mysterious and elfin, damn her, people always ask me if I have a headache. She's neither Neopagan nor Craft, and she runs the closest thing to a salon New York has seen since Edith Wharton stopped writing. I pushed open her living room door.

Cindy has a table made from one of those twelve-foot doors scavenged from some old East Side mansion. On Saturdays it's covered with food, with a tea urn at one end and coffee at the other. Nobody has ever been able to figure out why she does this.

You would think, with a free and semipublic spread, the place would be jammed, but it isn't. People who don't fit in hardly ever come back twice. I think Cindy changes them into toads.

(This is a joke. The only documented case of mantic theriomorphism on record is Aleister Crowley's turning a friend of his into a camel on one of their Near East walking trips, and Crowley lied.)

I came in and got tea. Cindy was sitting on a pile of pillows surrounded by her intimates. She looked like a punk Germaine de Stael.

I've never really been able to figure out whether I'm "in" Cindy's crowd. I think I'm the only Witch who hangs out at Cindy's, but I'm not sure about that either.

Another thing you learn to live with in New York is uncertainty.

I found a seat and sat. The conversation turned on the usual topics: bands I didn't know, books I hadn't read, scandals where I couldn't name any of the players. I fared slightly better when talk entered the World of Publishing: There the talk was all about who was (a) printing or (b) designing what magical book and what (c) lawsuits or (d) supernatural manifestations were attendant on that. Eventually I worked my way into an eddy in the conversation.

"I've really started getting interested in Russia, lately. You know, the pre-Christian magical system there?"

Neglect to substitute the codephrase "Pre-Christian religion" for "Paganism" in circles like these and you may be forced to listen for up to half an hour to someone telling you that Pagans do not exist. I've also heard that said about gremlins.

"Do you know anybody into that?" I kept saying, and eventually I struck paydirt.

"His name's Ruslan."

The speaker looked vaguely familiar and I finally placed him—he'd come to the Crossing circle last night. Fortunately for my peace of mind he'd left almost immediately afterward—hours before I had. He couldn't be my midnight tailer.

"He's into stuff like that."

"The guy up in Queens?" I said. *"Baba Yaga?"*

"Yeah." My informant relaxed, having fallen for the oldest trick in the book—the one about pretending you know more than you do. Convinced I already knew everything he was telling me, my new friend Damien told how Ruslan had moved into the area (New York Metropagan Community) and started working Russian. "Very shamanic," he said—which probably meant drugs used in Circle. Damien had only gone as far as the one visit, since what they wanted—"that secrecy shit and all"—was "too heavy" for him.

Cindy'd heard of *Baba Yaga*, too, and nailed down the reference for me.

"It's named after that evil sorceress who has a hut that walks around on chicken feet: Baba Yaga. The one who eats children. Like in *Fantasia*."

The things people think are in a harmless little movie never cease to amaze me. The same people who take their kids to see *Batman Returns* think the "Night on Bald Mountain" sequence from a fifty-year-old Disney film is corrupting our young.

Besides, I saw *Fantasia* again on its last release. There's no chicken feet in it anywhere.

I stayed another couple of hours at Cindy's but I didn't get anything else at all useful, if you don't count a couple of leads on who might need some freelance layout work done for them by someone who doesn't freak out at the sight of a pentacle.

But I had enough to annoy me. There was a coven in Queens that had been running for about a year. It was named after a black Witch in a Russian fairy tale, who was intimately connected with chicken feet a little bigger than the one Miriam had been wearing around her neck. Its leader's name was Ruslan, and it was a good bet he was the leader of the group that Miriam had been working with when she died.

6

S o here it was Monday again, and just about
ten days since Miriam died. As an avenging
angel I was a bust.

Belle'd called me Sunday night. The usual
thing—how was I, how were things, was I still
going unreasonably apeshit over Miriam's death.

I told her death was a part of the Great Cycle
of Rebirth. I did not tell her about any death
threats I may have received, or that there might
be a black coven in Queens murdering people. It
sounded stupid even to me, and Belle is so
laissez-faire she makes Ayn Rand look like a
Commie. If I told her everything I knew about
the *Baba Yaga*s Belle'd want to invite them to
Circle.

So she talked and I didn't, and she reminded
me that Changing was meeting again this Friday
and would I be sure to be there?

Belle only makes these special quality-time
phone calls to people she suspects may be in
need of them. I did not like the feeling of being

considered needy. I was supposed to be "over" Miriam by now—that much was plain.

But now it was Monday and I had a cup of truly awful coffee at my elbow and a razor blade between my fingers and a spread in front of me where the repro was in so many pieces that it resembled a ticker-tape collage. And Miriam wouldn't go away.

The ancient Greeks (who, as the Discordian saying goes, were in the sorry position of not being able to borrow any of their philosophy from the ancient Greeks) made dramatic hay from the idea that the blood of the murdered cries out for action on the part of the survivors—a literal, decibel-measurable crying that literally had to be done something about or nobody would get any sleep.

I envied the ancient Greeks. They at least had a murder or two in hand. I didn't have anything, except a line on some probably unpleasant people that my backbrain was trying to work out a way to meet.

I put in a long day at Houston Graphics/The Bookie Joint, first trying to jack up the old paycheck, then on a freelance piece of my own. It was after eight but still light when I left the studio.

It was the end of June, but the worst of the summer heat was still to come. It was pleasant enough that I decided to walk instead of taking the subway.

I often wonder, when I'm trying not to think about other things, if the citizens of Atlantis ever had any more idea that they were living at the pinnacle of civilization than the average New Yorker has. New York has been called "the only city" and "the new Atlantis" in about equal measure. Maybe it is: so big, complex, and information-packed that when people have really evolved to fit it they won't really be like other people anymore.

And then again, maybe sometime all the city services will go on strike at once and we won't have to worry about evolving any more.

My answering machine was flashing when I got home around nine: brilliant self-referential paragraphs of vermilion Morse that told me *lots* of people wanted to talk to me. I cranked up the volume and hit "Play."

Sometimes my capacity for self-abuse frightens me.

Lace, who left her name but no message. Somebody for High Tor Graphics (me), who left a message but no name. A couple of hang-ups, faithfully recorded. Someone trying to sell me the Sunday *New York Times* (an automated random-dialer). Tollah, calling from the Revel, and could I please read Tarot down at the shop on Saturday because their regular reader was having a crisis? More hang-ups. It's a good thing answering machines don't get bored.

Pay dirt.

The tone, then: "My name is Ruslan. I believe we have a number of friends and interests in common. I do hope you'll call me. My number is—" he rattled off a string of digits in 718, which is, among other things, Queens.

Nothing is ever gained by hasty action. I went and found the cassette I'd recorded Miriam's last message onto and added Ruslan's. I wrote down the phone number and tucked the cassette away again. I took the little Khazar missal out of my purse and looked at it.

There's a kind of phone book called the Criss-Cross Directory. Most libraries carry the one for their area. Instead of the usual alphabetic listings of Ma-Bell-as-was, all the phone numbers of your area are listed in numerical order, followed by who has them and where.

So if you have a phone number, you can get a name and address. If I took this phone number down to the New York Public on Forty-second Street, I'd bet more than a nickel it would go to the address in Queens I'd visited Saturday.

Bast, Girl Detective.

I hesitated between coffee and a beer and settled for tea. While I was waiting for the teabag to commit hygroscopia, I got out Miriam's last occult diary and turned to where I'd been using it to make notes on things Khazar. Under my notes on what Julian had said and what I'd heard at Cindy's, I added my first impressions of Brother Ruslan.

"I believe we have a number of friends and interests in common."

Ruslan had what is inaccurately referred to as a "white" voice—i.e., one that has been educated out of ethnic and regional identifiers. Not as common in New York as you might think; it'll soon be a thing of the past, but you can still frequently tell the borough, and sometimes the religion, of New Yorkers through vowels alone.

"I do hope you'll call me."

Yes, an educated voice. Maybe overeducated—just a little bit trying-too-hard to be upper-crust. *Look how very important and refined I am.*

It was familiar. Not the voice itself, but the *kind* of voice. I sat and drank my tea and stared out my only window while the light slid down toward *l'heure bleu.*

It was a professional voice. Doctor, lawyer, tax accountant, one of those fields that attracts bullies and sadists and emotional basket cases who have about as much compassion as a paper cup. An "I can do whatever I want, and not only are you helpless to stop me, if you don't pretend to trust me I am going to stick it to you even worse" voice.

Paranoid ravings aside, during the course of your schooling most professions slap a thin veneer of whitespeak over the vowels you were born with, and most professionals pretend to an infallibility that God Herself couldn't cop to once they get out into the world.

Guesses.

Was it the same voice as whoever called me the night before the Crossing circle? I thought about it hard and honestly and decided I'd never be sure. It wasn't impossible, though.

And if the mystery caller wasn't Ruslan, it was a safe bet the caller knew Ruslan and had handed over my unlisted phone number. Which Ruslan had chosen to call now.

I felt like the heroine around Chapter Seven of a horror novel, at the point where she dimly suspects she's the victim of several interlocking conspiracies, but doesn't know who's in them or how they fit together. Why should Ruslan call at all? Why now? What did he know—and what did he think I knew?

A professional voice. Doctor, lawyer, accountant . . . priest.

There was no help for it. I picked up the phone.

Ring, ring, ring . . .

"Hello?" The same voice, but a little more rough-edged.

"I'm returning Ruslan's call," I said and waited.

"Oh hey, *Karen*," Ruslan blossomed into polished talk-show sincerity. "*Hi.* How ya *doing*?"

I thought over which of my many personae to plug in to keep him talking. I decided on Pathetically Grateful, which someone with a voice like that would want everyone to be.

"*Hi,*" I emoted. "I'm so *glad* you *called.*"

Dead silence, while both of us listened to the conversational ball roll under the sofa. Columbo never has this problem.

"Well, I Knew you were trying to reach us. I was meditating, and I just . . . Heard you. I can always tell when someone's ready to Find us. So I called."

It was pure snake oil, delivered in the hushed pluralistic undertone of a mortician with a tapeworm. The next thing he'd do would be to remind me that my number was unlisted, so I could marvel at how he'd called anyway.

"Karen? Don't be afraid," he said reverently.

Pathetically Grateful took the bit in her teeth, which was a good thing, as left to my own personality I'd simply have hung up.

"Oh, no!" I agreed. "It's just that this . . ." I trailed off. I hoped he knew what I meant. I didn't.

"Miriam told me about you and how much you were into things like this—and I bet she told you a little about us, too."

It was a minute before I recognized the tone: Rogueishly Playful, with just a hint of "We're all boys / girls / little - green - furry - things - from - Alpha-Centauri here together."

I hated him. It was pure, primal, instinctive. It was also getting in my way.

"Miriam?" I said blankly.

There was a pause. It was a lot harder to string total strangers along into making Damning Confessions on the telephone than it looked in the books. "I mean, I *knew* Miriam. . . ." I added.

"Life and Death are in the Hands of the Gods," Ruslan intoned, tabling the question of what Miriam had or hadn't told me.

"I don't know what Miriam could have told you about me. I know she's been with a lot of groups. I'm in a group now, but I'm really looking for someone to study with who's more *shamanic*," I babbled on. And may Goddess have mercy on me if Belle ever found out what thumping lies I was telling.

"Perhaps Miriam mentioned the sort of things we do," Ruslan said. Fishing again, I realized.

"I'm really into *northern* things," I said, ignoring the hint. "Look, do you think it would be possible for me to visit your group? Are you open?"

Language is a wonderful thing. A translation into English of what I'd said so far in Paganspeak would go like this: *I'm interested in working with a magical group that uses drugs and related physical discipline to produce altered states of consciousness, but I'm not interested in anything Native American or related to Ceremonial Magic. Is your group currently accepting new members, and do I sound interesting/safe enough to you for you to let me come and see if I want to join you?*

"Some people think we're a little hierarchical," Ruslan said. (If you aren't willing to follow orders, forget it.)

"I think I'm ready for that. It's important to me to be with a group that's serious." (Just try me.) "I think I was meant to find you." (Remember who called whom.)

"I think you're right, Karen. Why don't you come over on Wednesday, around seven? You know where it is, don't you?"

Subtle as a truck.

"Well," I said coyly, "I don't know *exactly* . . . Somebody told me you were in Queens?" (You and I are both creatures of great occult power, of course, and I will admit I could find you by following your psychic emanations as long as you don't ask me to prove it.)

Finally Ruslan gave up trying to get me to admit Miriam had told me anything and reeled off a set of directions that sounded just like the ones she'd written down. Probably he did this a lot.

"We'll go out to dinner, and afterward maybe you can stay for the Circle." (Providing we like what we see, of course.)

"I'm looking forward to it," I said.

I hung up and stared at the phone for a long time.

My name is Bast.

That was the name Miriam had known me by. As far as I knew, she'd never heard of Karen.

Just who had supplied the information about Karen Hightower to Ruslan?

7

Seventy percent of all reported UFO sightings occur on a Wednesday. This particular Wednesday I was sitting on an uptown subway with no air-conditioning getting ready to meet Baba Yaga. I was being careful—at least I thought I was.

There was a letter in my apartment. I'd debated between addressing it to Belle or to Miriam's sister—neither of whom would do anything, I realized, so I addressed it to Belle, she should live and be well. At least I wouldn't have to tell her what all the words meant.

First impressions count for as much in the Community as anywhere. I didn't know if Ruslan knew anything at all about me (then why had he called?), but I didn't want to look either too amateurish or too professional. I left off all my funky in-group "kick me" jewelry and wore silver rings in the holes in my ears and my lesbian clusterfuck necklace around my neck—the one that you have to stare at for quite a long time before you realize it's entirely made up of women being nude and naughty. Black silk T. Black dress pants that (I fondly believed) made me look like a slumming runway model. My one set of really upscale footwear—a pair of black suede boots I'd blown an entire freelance commission's pay on at Bloomie's on sale.

I'd brought cash and tokens to cover the evening and left my purse at home, along with everything else that would tell Ruslan who I was and how much money I made. Was I a slumming yuppie? An upscaling waitress? Did I spend more time in the New York Public Library than he did? He wouldn't be able to tell by looking.

Never tell me the early Christians did not have these problems. After all, they used to worship naked, too.

Ruslan met me at the subway stop.

"Karen," he said. "So good to see you. Ruslan." This last in case I hadn't noticed the immense aura of magical power around him.

Ruslan was about average height, maybe an inch shorter, say five-ten. My boots had two-inch heels, which made me about as tall as he was. He didn't like it. He had that light hair that's neither brown nor blond, and pale blue eyes, and the kind of build that isn't quite fat but makes you think of something prize and pampered and well fed with ribbons on its halter. He was wearing an open-collared white dress shirt with jeans; he had a sterling silver belt buckle of a wolf biting the moon with a lot of

Cyrillic around it. The buckle looked expensive and custom.

His hands were short and blunt, almost like paws. I shook one of them.

"And this is my lady, Ludmilla."

"We're so pleased to meet you, Karen."

Ludmilla looked like someone had jammed her head between two books and squeezed—a piranha caught halfway through a transformation into a guppy. Pale bulging eyes and hair barely dark enough to be called brown. She wore it parted ruler-straight down the middle of her head and hanging down. She couldn't be old enough to have worn it that way as a teenager. Or maybe she could. It was hard to tell.

Ludmilla was wearing one of those expensive organic dresses—Laura Ashley or something like it—makeup, nylons, heels, and a suspicious lump on her left breast that might be a chicken foot stuffed into her bra. Her voice had a nasal out-of-town rasp I couldn't immediately place.

"I'm happy to be here," I said. Ruslan clapped me on the shoulder. I felt like I'd joined Rotary.

"I know this great restaurant," Ruslan said.

The restaurant turned out to be Turkish, or Armenian, or at least dark. The waiters all knew my hosts, which was how I found out that Ludmilla was Mrs. Ruslan, which implied that Ruslan had a first name somewhere. He kept calling me "Karen" at frequent intervals, like someone who has been too long in the thrall of Norman Vincent Peale.

Ruslan ordered for all three of us in the tone that's all smiles until you contradict it.

The food was good.

And I realized I was going to have to confess. *Everyone* confesses when they meet someone new. The story of their life. When they knew they were different. Trying to find God in all the places the approved sources say to, and finally deciding the sources are cruel or crazy because they tell you to go stand in this building where a bunch of men reel off centuries of rote words and they tell you this is God, this is religion, this is all there is of the not-human that interests itself in Man.

The Firesign Theatre had an album once: *Everything You Know Is Wrong.* Once you've found that out, been lied to that comprehensively, you look at everything a little more closely, trying to find out what other lies all the blind ones around you are accepting. And there're lots of blind ones and they're all happy and content and you're not and it gets damned lonely.

So when you find someone else who maybe, *maybe,* knows what it's like to wake up one day and realize everyone else is playing Let's Pretend, you talk.

I couldn't quite bring myself to do that. I fenced in the inarticulate *patois* of the nineties, that dialect where if the other person doesn't already know what you're saying he'll never find out by listening.

"Well, I came to New York a few years ago, you know, searching? I don't know if you *know.*

And I never was really comfortable with a lot of the stuff people were into, you know, when I *found out.* They seemed, well, like they weren't taking what they were into *seriously?*" I poked at my something-with-lamb-and-lemon.

"Most people don't," Ruslan intoned. I'd learned by now that he had two speeds—jovial and oracular. Jovial was like being French-kissed by a bulldozer. Oracular made me want to turn atheist. "Even those who should know better don't realize that they are meddling with living archetypes of immense power."

And there are things that man was not meant to know, I finished silently. And I thought about being someone with that desperate need for belonging and validation and knowing I wasn't just alone and making things up—and finding Ruslan.

"I didn't think anyone else understood," I said.

"It isn't especially easy," he admitted. "A great man once said that the first thing one must give up in order to study magic is the fear of insanity."

"Dessert?" said our waiter.

Apparently I could be trusted to order that by myself. I had the baklava and Ludmilla had the galactobourkia. The waiter looked at Ruslan.

"Now, Love," Ludmilla said. Ruslan shook his head. The waiter departed.

"I have to watch what I eat," he said. A little defensively, I thought.

"Ruslan has these *shamanic trances,*" Ludmilla explained proudly.

A fact that you may have forgotten if you live in one of the major population centers is that women's liberation, The Revolution, has not yet been universal. It seemed that Ludmilla Ruslan adhered to the older, purer doctrine—that of full-time cheering section for the man of her choice.

This is not a good way to be. If it's unilateral, it's degrading. If it's reciprocal, it's nauseating.

Think about it. If you had "shamanic trances," would *you* tell the world?

I turned back to Ruslan. "You go into trance?" I said, hoping I looked fascinated.

He smiled. Of course he'd wanted to be asked. Another thing an old-fashioned girl is good for is providing a straight line.

"Started when I was a boy. I was pretty severely diabetic, so I used to be sick a lot of the time. And when I'd go into coma I'd have these *experiences*. Nothing like them in the literature. And strange things would happen when I woke up. So I started trying to understand them, and I realized that the shock to my system was actually projecting my astral self into the shamanic dreamtime."

I looked politely impressed. It might even be true. I'd heard weirder things from people who were perfectly sincere about it. The religious urge itself is bizarre enough; after that it's all quibbling. The question was not "Is the story intrinsically unbelievable?" but, "Does *Ruslan* believe it?"

Or was he lying, and if so, why?

"I realized it was important for me to learn all

that I could about the dreamtime, so I could learn to guide others." Ruslan smiled. Ludmilla looked proud.

I had a sudden snapshot image, vivid as a cliché: the Russian steppes, flat as the plains of Kansas and a thousand times wider, salt-white with ice under a sky as blue as midnight. Chiaroscuro moon and fat white stars unwinking in the airless vault.

Ruslan's dreamtime, as offered to his acolytes.

"Yes," I said.

On the walk back from the restaurant to the house I delivered to myself a stern mental lecture on not being a self-abnegating romantic jackass. Ruslan had a good line of patter, and he wasn't exactly the first to decide that post-Bomb America is a culture romancing oblivion. People have always worshiped what scared them, on the plausible theory that if they were nice enough to it, it would go away. The gods of agriculture and husbandry are the gods of famine. The gods of love are the gods of rejection.

What was it Julian had called Ruslan's theme? Ecological nihilism? The flirtation with the ultimate terror—extinction.

So Ruslan had a good line of patter. Fine. If that was all he had, that was fine, too. Miriam hadn't killed herself; I wasn't here because I thought he'd talked her into suicide.

I was here because Miriam had asked me to help. And because if she were still alive, I'd be here, gathering my own facts in order to be fair.

* * *

We went back to the apartment, so I guessed I'd passed the initial interview and would get to see an actual episode of Russian Shamanic Wicca. Even though I was nine-tenths certain that Nothing Was Going To Happen I had damp palms and a dry mouth standing there in front of the door while Ruslan dragged out his keys. Suppose they dragged me inside and cut me up with a chain saw? Suppose his whole group was waiting inside with sterling silver icepicks? Suppose—

I'm sure the Lone Ranger never felt this way.

Ruslan opened the door, and the only thing waiting for me was a cloud of stale Russian Church incense. Ruslan's apartment smelled just like Miriam's apartment. Ludmilla turned on the lights.

"Why don't I just go and make some tea— people ought to be arriving in about half an hour."

Ludmilla bustled off across the living room. I looked around.

I don't know every practicing Neopagan in America, but I've been in a lot of living rooms, in New York and out. Rich, poor, and in between, they all have a certain family resemblance that comes of being decorated by a bunch of people coming from the same microculture, with the same assumptions about the world.

Ruslan's didn't.

It wasn't just that there weren't Sierra Club posters on the wall, or that there *were* large pictures of the Sacred Heart of Jesus. It was something subtler. A sense of priority.

It was a big apartment—big by New York standards, meaning that it had a separate kitchen, through the doorway to which I could hear Ludmilla bashing the tea things about. There were doors leading off both sides of the living room; two bedrooms, probably.

The living room furniture was stylish and modern and new-but-not-good. Vinyl couch, glass-and-brass tables—Monkey Ward's copies of *Architectural Digest* originals. Abstract geometric rugs in earth tones, from the same source. No books in sight. The only honest things in the room were the paintings.

There were twelve of them, about eighteen by twenty-four, done on wood in Russian lacquerwork style and hung without frames. They were done by the same artist who had done Miriam's missal.

They were not nice. But I wondered, as I looked at them, if I would have disliked them so much if I didn't already dislike Ruslan.

"What do you think?"

"They're very well done."

"Thank you. My own work." That much was an honest reaction. "Of course, I'm not a professional. A number of people have said I should do more, and of course I've exhibited, but it would take too much time away from my real work." A line of patter so standard I could parse it in my sleep.

"They're beautiful." I felt something warmer was called for, even if I do always get irritated

with myself when I lie. They weren't beautiful—
not even with the romantic Gothic "terrible
beauty" of an advancing lava flow. They were
just *there*, inimical as a beaker of cyanide.

I stepped closer to the pictures.

"I paint in blood," Ruslan said behind me. I
turned around and caught the sadistic good-ol'-
boy gleam in his eye. He expected me to be
freaked out. That was why he'd told me. To
watch me squirm and then apologize for squirm-
ing.

"Yours?" I asked politely.

His face went completely blank for a moment;
then he laughed and I saw him abandon his cat-
and-mouse game for the moment. When he
spoke again it was almost a non sequitur.

"I'm very drawn to the Russian archetypes.
The Khazar people were a vital and important
Pagan culture that flourished in the Black Sea
area around the second millennium B.C.E.
When Christianity was introduced by the ruling
classes as a means of disenfranchising the in-
digenous Pagan tribes, they embedded the vital
images of Khazar religion in their own mythol-
ogy. I'm trying to reclaim them so that the eastern Slavic peoples can once again practice their
native tradition," Ruslan orated.

We were back on track with Pagan Indoctri-
nation Lecture #4-B. Nobody wants to be the
one to start something, especially a religion.
There are two ways of handling this: Either say
you are actually reviving a religion that fell into
disuse longer ago than anybody can remember
(that's how Judaism started; read your Bible), or

say you are reforming the one that's already there (Christianity, which started as Reform Judaism; and Protestantism, which began as Reform Catholicism).

Even in Wicca someone is always unearthing a Book of Shadows that belonged to his great-grandmother, which is always exactly like most of the others that have been published, the first of which can be documented as having been written circa 1953.

"I've always been fascinated with Old Russia," I said, turning my back on the pictures painted in blood. I was saved from parading my ignorance by Ludmilla's arrival with a big tolework tray: tall glasses full of black tea; sugar lumps and cherry preserves; right out of Chekhov. The *folklorico-manqué* clashed just a trifle with the Levittown *moderne.*

"Sugar or jam?" chirped Ludmilla brightly, dropping a big glop of cherries into her glass. The glass rested in a little brass basketwork holder with a ring-shaped handle down near the bottom. It looked more like a candleholder than anything else, and like a perfect way for Bast to slop boiling tea on herself.

"Sugar," I said. "Is there milk?" I was deliberately not picking up on their cues for in-group bonding, and I could see it was putting Ruslan just a little off balance.

"We're going to have to teach you to drink tea like a Khazar!" he said in a hearty-sinister voice, but in all fairness I would have found a discussion of the weather sinister by then.

"Now, Love," Ludmilla said. "There's milk in the refrigerator, Karen; I'll—"

"Oh, I can get it." I was already standing, and the buzzer buzzed, so Ludmilla went to let who-ever-it-was in and I went off to the kitchen.

I did not poke around, but I kept my eyes open. When I opened the refrigerator I saw a lineup of little bottles in the egg-holders in the door that nobody uses for eggs. Insulin. The name on the prescription label was Michael Ruslan.

One thing verified. He *was* a diabetic.

I heard voices in the living room. I came back with the milk and poured it in my tea and made meaningless friendly noises at the two men and a woman who'd come in. Max, Norris, and Star-fawn, if I heard the mumbles right.

"And what's your name?" Starfawn said. She was small, round, and young—younger than any of the rest of us by a good ten years. Twenty-two, maybe.

"Jadis," I said firmly, before Ruslan could introduce me. "That's my magical name," I added. I thought it would be a good idea to es-tablish my alias early on, and I didn't think I'd have trouble sounding plausible to a woman who had chosen to be known to her gods as Starfawn.

"Hey, right on," said either Max or Norris.

"It's a good strong name," said Ruslan.

It should be—I'd stolen it from the witch-queen of *Narnia.* Ludmilla took the milk carton back into the kitchen. I looked down at my tea.

The milk had settled about a half inch below the surface, like a ball of taffy dropped in ice water.

There was a short awkward time after that. Ludmilla brought out more tea. A couple more people arrived—I was glad not to see anybody I knew—and the talk skittered nervously around Baba Yaga secrets; things they couldn't discuss in front of an outsider.

It was probably mostly entirely harmless stuff. If it had been any normal coven I would have known that for sure—it would have been about magical healings, divinations, the usual small talk of a busy extended family. Here I didn't know what to think.

Ruslan ran the conversation. He didn't say much once the company arrived, but the others had a tendency to look at him before they spoke and several times he corrected their opinions.

Starfawn was the one edited most often.

"Are we going to do anything else about S—" she began.

"Secrecy builds power," Ruslan said, looking pointedly at me. "Jadis hasn't taken an oath, Starfawn."

Starfawn's cheeks went pink and she looked away.

"That's quite all right," I said. Do anything else about who? S. Sunshrike? *Miriam?*"

Whether they could do it or not, simply thinking about dragging someone back from the Summerland was so unethical my teeth hurt. But they hadn't wanted her to reach it, had they?

They'd wanted her to wander through the outer dark forever.

"Oh, what a cute necklace!" Starfawn squealed, fastening her gaze on my chest full of intertwined sterling *frottagistes*.

They might be clowns, but nasty ones.

Eventually everyone was there—ten people, including me—and we got down to the serious business of the evening. There were no coed dressing or undressing rooms; in fact, Baba Yaga worked robed, and I was shuttled off to the bedroom with Starfawn, Ludmilla, and two other women to dress.

I kept my eyes open, just as I had in the kitchen. The bedroom had the same distressing air of mundanity that the living room had had. The only thing even remotely out of the ordinary was the neat pile of boxes in the corner. I took a closer look. The boxes were still sealed, bedight with "Fragile" and "Flammable" stickers, and had been shipped to Michael Ruslan at Clean-O-Rama, somewhere in Queens.

People's day jobs are lousy for the soul of true Romance. Here he was, Ruslan the Great, freelance prince of darkness; by day a mild-mannered laundromat owner. Sure.

"*Here* you are, Karen," Ludmilla sang out. She was holding a bundle of white muslin out toward me.

I stripped down to my Jockey for Hers and put it on. The fabric was scratchy and had a harsh chemical smell that I was determined to ignore. Mothballs? It had a white drawstring sash, and when I looked in the mirror I saw an overaged refugee from Santa Lucia Night.

Everyone else had on black robes. I remembered Miriam's robe with its careful embroidery. I'd thought about bringing it, but I was glad now that I hadn't gotten cute. The black robes were enlivened by varying degrees of ornamentation, and when the ladies were all suited up the bedroom looked like a cross between a medievalist event and a Roman Catholic reunion.

Ludmilla's black velvet robe was accented by cuffs, cummerbund, and stola in some gaudy, glittery, patterned material. She had a string of antique amber beads around her neck I would gladly have committed several illegal acts to own, and her chicken foot was proudly displayed on its heavy silver chain. It was shriveled and yellow and looked like a depraved saint's relic.

To top everything off, Lady Ludmilla wore a weird little round hat on her head that made her resemble an escapee from a demented Victorian nursing school.

Status, wealth, and temporal power—all the things you're supposed to leave outside the circle. Not because they're evil. Because they get in the way. Maybe they didn't get in the way of whatever sort of ritual Ruslan's coven was used to.

When all five of us were tricked out in what the well-dressed Khazar—and sacrificial victim—will wear, we went back into the living room. I was glad I'd had the chance to see Ludmilla in all her glory first, because then when I saw Ruslan I didn't even blink.

They say that the "Reverend" Montague Summers used to dress up in full Roman Catholic regalia to attend afternoon tea—which is a case of costume inappropriate to the occasion, but not as much so as wearing the same drag to a Wiccan covenmeet.

Well, not quite the same. Ruslan had on the alb, the stola, and the embroidered gauntlets, and the hat that looks like a folded napkin, but there were no Christian symbols on them, just a lot of moons and stars and wolves painstakingly hand-embroidered by somebody else. He had on a long necklace of black beads that might very well have been jet.

He also wore a bird-footed pendant. I wasn't sure what bird had donated it—it was a little too small for an ostrich, though. He had a whatever the Baba Yaga call their *athames* sheathed at his waist.

He opened the door to the other bedroom and led us all into the temple.

If you're going to get picky about it, a temple is a permanent structure dedicated to the working of magic-with-a-*K*. Magicians have them. Pagans don't.

Oh, the *asatruer* in your life will have his *fane*, and the *mambo* his *hounfort*, but a coven is an *organization*, not a place. The place where it meets is the covenstead, but that's only a special name for a place, not a special place. Wherever a coven meets it builds its Circle, and when the meeting is over and the Circle is broken, there's nothing left behind to indicate anything extraordinary ever occurred there.

This was not the case with Ruslan's Khazar temple, which looked as if it owed more of its inspiration to the Russian Catholic Church than it did to the precepts of Gerald Gardner.

Julian's words about "the usual mishmash" came back to me again. The floor was painted with a full-dress Solomon's Seal after Francis Barrett's *The Magus*. It was done in four colors of deck paint and must have taken hours. The walls were painted in the elemental colors (Golden Dawn attribution) and hung with large painted satin banners with the Four Tools on them. There were four large candleholders at the cardinal points, each of which held a faintly oatmeal-colored candle weighing easily five pounds. Assorted icons, oil lamps, and ritual paraphernalia were hung from the hooks on the walls, giving the place something of the look of the Serpent's Truth's broom closet. The altar was set up in the center of the circle, and everything (still, so far,) looked normal.

At least to me. It had been years since I'd given a thought to walking into a situation like this with a group of more-or-less total strangers. I'd made my decision a long time ago, when I started chasing deity the way Harvard MBAs chase money.

Ludmilla lit the lamps on the walls and the lamps on the altar. I heard the subway rumble by outside as Ruslan shut and locked the door. That made me a little nervous, but it was his empowerment symbol, and a door locked from the side you're on can be got through easily. Ruslan proceeded to open the closet, and I could see packages of supplies, neatly labeled, inside.

Ludmilla made another pass around the room and lit the quarter-candles. I was standing next to the northern one; it smelled spicy and sweet as it burned. My skin under the robe itched.

Ruslan turned away from the closet and walked toward me.

"I thought you might like to borrow an *athame*, Kar—*Jadis*. We keep this one as a spare."

The smile was enough warning, but there wasn't anything I could do. He held it out and I took it.

It had about a six-inch blade, and the pommel was amber. An Ironshadow blade—there was his signature near the quillons. The edge of the pommel was rough and shiny where someone had taken a Dremel-tool and sanded Miriam's name off.

It felt like cold and death and pain and dying alone.

My stomach convulsed around my Lamb Surprise and tea and I swallowed hard, but Ruslan had already turned away from me. This was one reaction he didn't need to see to savor.

"Brothers and sisters of the Khazar, tonight we meet in worship of the Old Gods. With us is Jadis, a seeker, and out of respect to her, we will engage in worship only this evening."

He turned back to me. "I have to ask you to

respect our privacy, and ask you not to reveal anything you may see or hear tonight." He stared at me, his eyes as bright and horrid as if they were blue glass, and I clutched Miriam's *athame*, my gift to her, the one thing she would never have given willingly to anyone else.

I must have said something and it must have sounded normal. Ruslan went over to the altar and he and Ludmilla began the ritual.

The fondness of the Gardnerian tradition for incense is a standing joke in the Community, but the Baba Yagas went us one better that night. Ten minutes into the ritual the room was actually foggy, with a sharp, cloying smell I could taste. It reminded me vaguely of winter woolies, and closets, and things like that, and I found myself swaying back and forth just like everyone else. My eyes watered. I wondered if what the Khazars were burning on their charcoal was DEA-legal.

By the time they got around to passing the wine cup—what Belle always calls Sacred Cookies and Milk Time—I had a pounding headache. My mouth and throat were cottony and dry. We were all sitting on the floor with people swaying back and forth to that unheard music which is sweeter. Wolves and winter wind howled in the background, courtesy of a sound-system The Cat would have coveted.

All my energy was going into keeping the ritual from reaching me at the deep-mind level where it could fuck me up for years—that, and keeping from parting Ruslan's hair with one of his pretentious High Church candlesticks. If I'd wanted to go to Mass I would have stayed a nun.

My sinuses had given up long ago, and by now my eyes were watering so badly that Baba Yaga Her Own Self could have shown up and I wouldn't have been any the wiser. Despite my best efforts at insulating myself from what *Baba Yaga* and Ruslan were doing I had that unsettled, hair-prickling feeling of just-before-a-storm, and my skin felt like it was on inside out and backwards.

I trust my feelings. When the cup reached me I didn't drink.

Oh, I tilted it back, all right, but I kept my mouth tight shut and I was glad I had. The candles lit up some oily beads of non-wine liquid floating on the surface, and I got a caustic breath of something that cleared my sinuses and made my head ring. I held my breath and lowered the cup, and the person next to me took it away from me. I took a deep breath of camphor smoke and tried to stay upright. *Camphor*, I realized with a sense of how foggy I was. The candles were scented with camphor. Why?

The sense of something waiting got stronger. Again, there was no need of occult power to guess why. Most people don't realize how much of their information about other people is based on reading nonverbal cues. Their conscious mind offers it to them in the form of "feelings" or "hunches," and they promptly discount it as being irrational.

I didn't.

"It is usual, when one of us has gone to live in

the dreamtime forever, to release the last of their ties to the earth-plane," Ruslan said as soon as the cup had gone all the way around the room once. "But we haven't been able to do this for Sunshrike. Can you help us, Jadis? Karen?"

My head felt like it weighed a thousand pounds and was stuffed with white phosphorus. I had just enough brains left to realize I was blitzed and to be very, very careful of what I said.

"Can I help you," I repeated thickly. I was starting to realize how much earth-plane trouble I was in, and how unequipped I was to deal with it.

"Miriam had some things that belong to us. They're too dangerous to leave around loose. Weren't you in her apartment after she died?"

My thoughts turned into little heraldic salamanders, each orange and burning and with a pinpoint of sapphire brilliance lodged in its skull. Take that stone from the salamander and become impervious to fire—or use it to make the Philosopher's Stone, which turns lead into gold and makes men immortal.

I hadn't been in this condition for *years*.

"Karen? I know you were in Miriam's apartment after she died." Ruslan, standing there calm and magisterial. And why not? He was above the worst of the smoke, and I'd bet he hadn't had any of the wine. Everyone else in the room looked like bleary-eyed opium eaters, including Ludmilla.

"Won't you help us?"

Actually, I was willing to tell him anything to

make him go away. I had an unshakable conviction that he'd know if I didn't tell the truth.

But, damn it, I was High Priestess and Witch.
And Ruslan wasn't. I summoned up all my pride,
if nothing else.

"Miriam's apartment was burglarized," I said
carefully. My tongue felt like a cucumber. Bad,
bad violation of Craft ethics to use drugs in a
Circle without making sure everyone knew in
advance and could consent.

But they hadn't wanted me to know and to
consent. They'd wanted to get me to where they
could put the boot in. And I'd walked in just like
Mary's little lamb.

I'd made two mistakes that I wasn't ever
going to make again. I should have yelled a lot
longer and louder when Mr. Michael Ruslan
called up my unlisted number with my legal
name.

And I should never have assumed that "cov-
ener" meant "law abiding."

"Miriam was talking about leaving. She was
talking about showing those things to a friend of
hers. That's against the oath. If someone took
those things, they took Miriam's oath, too, and
the Babayar will find them wherever they are."

"Hunt them down," said Starfawn, slurrily.

I wanted to confess. I was going to confess, I
was almost sure of it, and then I was going to kill
him.

*Goddess Who art bound to me by oaths and
love, strengthen me now—*

Someone started to chant; a short sharp line
with a lot of plosives. The rest joined in; a condi-

tioned response as automatic as the "amen" at the end of a hymn. Ruslan smiled at me. The wolves on the "Environments" tape howled. In that room Ruslan's Babayar was as real as gravity, and I clenched my teeth to keep from making any noise at all.

"If you hear of anyone who might have Miriam's things, I'd really appreciate it," Ruslan said again.

We were back to reality. I was standing in Ruslan's living room, dressed in my own clothes. The clock showed 12:45 A.M., and people were standing around getting ready to leave.

My nose ran and my lungs hurt, and my (hand wash only silk) shirt was already soaked through with sweat. I had a putrid headache and was too miserable to be self-righteous or even to pitch my voice very loud. In addition, I wasn't sure where the last four hours had gone and I had the vague feeling of impending doom that comes from having made a serious mistake that you don't quite realize yet. I mumbled something.

"They're dangerous in the wrong hands. Miriam was trying to leave, and look what happened to her."

Even if it was fevered intuition, there was no mistaking his meaning. I stared at Ruslan. He smiled.

"Miriam wouldn't have died if she'd kept her oath. But you know that, Karen. Secrecy builds power. And power can be very dangerous when it turns against you. I think Miriam knows that now. Don't you?"

Someone opened the door to the apartment. I went through it without looking back.

8

THURSDAY, JUNE 28, 1:15 a.m.

This was not how it was supposed to go. I was supposed to be sure there was a murder and not know who did it. But I wasn't sure there had been a murder—and I had somebody confessing to it. Hell, *bragging* about it.

It was raining as I left the Ruslans' apartment, the peculiarly unpleasant thin warm summer-in-the-city stuff. I could feel the smog-in-solution coating my skin and ensuring that everything I had on would have to be dry-cleaned.

I felt that special light-headed gratitude that comes from having had a brush with death or root canal and surviving. I didn't even worry about being mugged on the platform as I waited for the downtown train. It was after midnight; the sky had that weird greenish underglow that comes from reflecting a lot of light. New York, the city that never sleeps.

And now I had my fact, my real-for-true undeniable fact. The fact I'd wanted, angled for, and gone out on a limb to get. Miriam's death was neither accidental nor coincidental. Michael Ruslan of the *Baba Yaga* Coven, Khazar Tradition, had motive and opportunity and swore he'd put them together and killed Miriam Seabrook.

With sorcery.

My train got there and I got in. The New York Transit Authority had kindly arranged for it to be air-conditioned to a level capable of dealing with the thermal output of its peak ridership, thereby guaranteeing that the after-midnight travelers had a good chance of catching pneumonia. It did nothing to improve my headache.

I shared my car with a couple of members of what is tactfully called these days the underclass—fat, dark, weary ladies wearing white and talking together in Spanish. Too close to poverty and reality to live in a world where people did things like Ruslan's guest-bedroom cathedral. The money he'd spent on the incense was a week's groceries in their world.

It's called innocence, and the distinction between it and ignorance is fast dying out.

Three stops later—at the first Manhattan stop—one of the joys of MTA ridership boarded. He was tall, white, and barefoot and wearing corrugated cardboard placards front and back. His head was wrapped in purple cellophane and he wore one of those bouncy antenna headbands that'd been hot a few years back. I couldn't read his sandwich boards. He carried a saxophone. As soon as the train was in motion and he had a captive audience, he started to play it.

Pontius Pilate wanted to know what truth was. If he'd just waited twenty centuries he could have given up on that one and started asking about sanity.

And how was the Sax Man different from Ruslan? Or for that matter, from me?

I got off the train near Rocky Center and walked over to an all-night coffee shop I knew. It had stopped raining by then and the streets were all black glass, shining and as deserted as Manhattan ever gets.

It was only when I saw the lights and people at the Cosmic Coffee Shop that I realized how badly I wanted both. I was shook all the way down to the prerational level that good ritual is designed to touch. And whatever else was true, the Baba Yagas knew how to make a ritual.

Of course, so had the Nazis.

I slid into a booth with the same sense of relief a player of Tag-You're-It feels reaching home.

I had coffee. I had white wine. I had scrambled eggs and home fries and I wanted a cigarette desperately, even though I'd only ever been an occasional smoker and that not for years. I bought a little metal box of Excedrin from behind the counter and took them all with a second glass of wine, and finally I was able to put down the feeling that a Stephen King Nightmare From The Id was waiting to drag me off into the fifth dimension.

Fact: Ruslan had said that *Baba Yaga* had killed Miriam for oathbreaking. But black magic wasn't illegal, even if it worked. Was it? I didn't think there was a jury in the world that would convict Ruslan of Miriam's death, even if he'd been serious. Plain and fancy bragging is a long-standing tradition in the Community, after all. *"Look what I healed, invoked, divined."* This was just bragging of a darker sort.

But in my heart I knew it wasn't. If intention counted, Ruslan had killed Miriam Seabrook.

The next question I had to ask myself was, *Had* he killed Miriam? Effective *malificarum* is rare in the world today—it's so much harder than calling your lawyer, and about as healthy for you as smoking crack.

It comes down in the end to what you believe. If you think, down in the dark night of your soul, that a person can die on command, and that another person can give them that command, then Ruslan *could* be guilty.

If the human mind can raise stigmata or cause hot coals not to burn, surely it can stop the human heart?

Can, not *had.* Ruslan *could* be guilty. *He* thought he was. But what if he was firing blanks?

And what if he wasn't?

The Roman Catholic Church used to distinguish between intending to do something wicked and actually getting around to it. They were both sins, of course, but there was a difference in degree. I sat in the diner and drank lots of coffee and thought deep philosophical thoughts about the exact moment at which a crime has been committed.

If there was an ecclesiastical court for the Craft, Ruslan was definitely guilty on a number of counts.

He was (I was pretty sure) using drugs in ritual without the prior informed consent of all participants.

He was engaged in invasive, coercive magic—what we used to call, in less enlightened days, Black Magic. Whether he had any success at it or not, he had "attempted to compass the death of the said Miriam Seabrook by nigromantic operations."

Fine. But it wasn't a civil crime—at least I didn't think there were any laws against *malificarum* on the books in the State of New York. The closest there were (and a real pain in the ass to people like Tollah and Tris) were the Gypsy Laws, which are designed to protect the moron in the street against fraud enacted by the palm-and-tea-leaf reading brethren.

Guilty or not, Ruslan had committed no temporal crime.

The question was, just how good was he at committing spiritual ones?

The jury was out on that one, but I took the proper precautions around the apartment anyway when I finally got there: from salt and iron to a blue candles ritual. By eight A.M. I had my apartment swept and garnished and psychically sealed, in as valid and practical a defense as Ruslan's could be an assault.

My wards were designed, as all good ethical magical systems are, to be purely passive; they would draw their energy from being attacked. If Ruslan wanted to take the trouble to hoodoo me, I wanted to make sure he got back what he sent, doubled and redoubled in spades.

Needless to say, it was not a night for sleeping.

But it was a day for earning a living, so later Thursday morning I washed the vervain and lemongrass and golden seal off in my dinky claustrophobic shower and got dressed and went down to the studio. My subconscious still had that overfed and undigested feel to it that meant it was just itching to bring things to my attention if left alone. I felt that I'd be happy to leave it alone for an equinoctial precession or two, along with Ruslan's nasty-minded godplayers and all the rest.

Because there was nothing I could do. And that was the unkindest truth of all.

Having missed a night's sleep didn't bother me—yet. But it would if I didn't make it up, and I had coven tomorrow night. So when I got into work that Thursday I told Raymond I'd be in late on Friday, planning to leave early and catch up on lost sleep, and then like a right jerk stayed overtime instead.

It was late. Everyone else was gone. It was nice and quiet and still light out, actually my favorite time of day to be here.

The phone rang.

You would think that the first thing on my

mind would be all the nasty phone calls I'd gotten lately, but my subconscious was too busy with other stuff to bother making my life miserable. I answered the phone without a qualm in my heart.

"Bookie-Joint-can-I-help-you?"

"It's Lace. I tried your apartment and there wasn't anybody there, so I thought . . ."

I resisted the flip and cowardly urge to ask her if somebody else was dead. "How are you?" I said instead.

"Oh, not too good. Tollah says you're coming down to read at the Revel on Saturday. Maybe you'd like to go out to dinner afterward. Shop'll pay."

This is not quite as magnanimous of Tollah as it might appear. I don't read Tarot for her very often, because while she splits the take fifty-fifty with her usual fortune-teller, I have an ethics problem with taking money for magic—so when I read, Tollah scoops the lot. Her conscience bothers her enough to feed me.

"Yeah, sure," I said, wondering why she called, and knowing why. There was a Miriam-sized hole in Lace's life, and I'd known Miriam, too. Lifelong relationships have been formed on less.

"Have you heard anything? About the autopsy, or . . . anything?" Lace said.

Autopsy.

Brain-fever struck, so hard I almost hung up on her. *CAMPHOR* I wrote in large letters on the top of my board and underlined it three times.

Camphor in the candles. Ether (or something) in the cup. Drugs.

Poisons.

"Hello?" said Lace, after a minute. "Hello? Bast?"

"I'm here." The patter of little feet that was my subconscious doing a tap dance of joy at finally getting my attention was deafening. "No, I haven't heard anything more about the autopsy."

"What about the *Baklava* people?" Lace asked with unerring precision.

"I just talked to them," I admitted, wondering how I was going to edit my experience to keep Lace from going after Ruslan with a baseball bat.

And I *was* going to keep her from doing that, because as much as I wanted justice, I wanted even more not to be responsible even slightly for some kind of "Commie Satanist from Mars" story in the *New York Post,* with Lace stuck in the middle of it. We're edging up on the millennium, and newspapers have always had a bit of trouble distinguishing between "Neopagan" and "Nut."

"Look. I really can't talk right now. But I'll tell you all about it on Saturday, okay? Really, they're mostly harmless."

So's a rattlesnake.

I spent another ten minutes soothing Lace down before I could hang up, and then I flew on wings of song to one of the bookshelves where the fruits of Houston Graphics' labors are stored.

A studio like Houston, which handles (let's face it) the leftovers and bits-and-pieces that fall through the cracks of the big studios and the publishers' in-house art departments, does a little of everything. We've mechanicaled pornography, haute fantasy, how-to books, technical manuals, medical textbooks, and everything else under the sun—including the monster *World Encyclopedia of Wine* (all nine hundred pages) that comes in for a complete patch-and-fit job every time somebody comes up with a new way to spell Chablis.

And usually the publisher sends us a couple copies of the book when it comes off press, which explains why the walls at Houston Graphics resemble a library gone wrong.

When you stare at something day after day you can hardly help reading it, which is why I know as much about diagnostic approaches to cardiopulmonary resuscitation as I do. And I'd read something, sometime, about camphor. And ether.

The book was called *A Poison Dictionary*. It was one of those helpful reference books wherein a technical subject is demythologized for the layman, and the consensus at Houston was that it was written so Middle America would be able to off troublesome spouses and children with ease. It was a trade paperback with a (you should pardon the expression) poison-green cover and an alphabetical list of "over 1,000 common household substances" that could be fatal.

Some of them were very weird. I mean, aspirin? *Coffee?*

And Vicks VapoRub (used incorrectly, of course, as the entry was very careful to point out). Or to put it another way, *camphor.*

If it doesn't kill you, said the book, camphor induces, along with your headache, excitement, dizziness, and irrational behavior—though the book didn't mention what it considered irrational behavior. I made a note of the page number and kept on looking, because the candles hadn't killed Miriam.

The wine had.

Consider what you want out of life if you're some kind of charlatan working the occult circuit. You probably don't believe in magic, but you want your followers to believe in you, and you want to be sure they are docile, biddable, and experience Real Occult Manifestations they can brag to their friends about.

In the Middle Ages, it was easy. The so-called Witches' Flying Ointment used a combination of belladonna (nightshade, water parsley), bufotenin (toad sweat), digitalis (foxglove), and aconite (wolfsbane) to achieve these useful effects. As compounded from medieval recipes and tested by modern researchers (some people will do anything for a government grant), W.F.O. produces the sensation of flying, a feeling of exhilaration— and a set of three-ring hallucinations that may have accounted for most of the more lurid depositions people like Spengler and Kramer collected during the witch trials. Oh, people believed they'd been to the Sabbat, all right—

with that particular chemical cocktail coursing through their blood, how could they not?

But this is now. And if you wanted to get the same effects in the modern coven, those particular ingredients were pretty hard to come by.

But ether wasn't. Or chloroform.

Especially if your day job involved a Clean-O-Rama—or any other place that might handle dry cleaning. The boxes in the bedroom suddenly made a horrible kind of sense. Both ether and chloroform are used in dry cleaning. Anybody with a plausible excuse and a credit card can get his hands on them quite easily.

Chloroform. A mildly caustic gaseous anesthetic, I read in *A Poison Dictionary*, liquid when chilled, gaseous at slightly above room temperature. It would burn your mouth if you drank it, but mixed with the sacramental wine you probably wouldn't notice much. A whiff would give you a dizzy, floaty, out-of-body feeling—add that to the camphor in the candles and the hypnostasis of the ritual and you would be sure that in Russian Orthodox Wicca you had found something with more bang for your buck than spending Sunday morning down at the First Methodist Bar & Grill.

Ingest enough chloroform over a period of time and it would kill you. Cirrhosis. Necrosis. Your liver stops working and you die. Without warning. Real fast. Alone, in a locked room, miles away from your killer.

My hands were shaking so hard I dropped the book. I crawled under my table to get it and rang my head on the underside of my board.

Getting out seemed like too much trouble so I just sat there, reading over the entry again.

Chloroform causes liver failure. And there had been chloroform or its next-door neighbor in the wine. Ruslan had put it there.

Motive, opportunity, and access to tools. There was a real-world cause of Miriam's death—and if I could prove it, I could nail Ruslan with manslaughter, voluntary or in-.

But if he used that stuff on a regular basis, why wasn't everyone in Ruslan's coven dead?

The dictionary—admittedly not the most reliable source in the universe—cited repeated doses—or overdoses—as cause of death-by-chloroform. Maybe other people *had* died. Maybe the police were closing in even now, their dragnet drawing ever tighter around *Baba Yaga* and its High Priest.

Or maybe Miriam had just come up unlucky.

But would she have been quite so unlucky, I wondered, if *Baba Yaga* hadn't been working magic to cause her death?

I took the book with me when I left the studio. Ray wouldn't miss it, and I wanted to think— about it and everything else in the world.

Miriam Seabrook was dead. And Ruslan was at one and the same time a vicious and merciless committer of premeditated murder and an irresponsible goof who thought it was cute to slip people drugs without their knowing.

Just about everybody my age either knows someone it happened to or had it happen to them: the LSD in the orange juice, the hashish in the brownies, the magic mushrooms in the scrambled eggs. Back in the sixties, when drugs were supposed to be powerful and liberating and upscale things, these were harmless pranks—at least people said so.

But heroin moved out of the ghetto and cocaine moved into the marketplace and about the time your local pusher's daily special was something that would kill you before it addicted you, drugs stopped being cute.

But some of us were still hanging on to all of the sixties we could. And maybe Ruslan was one of them and still thought of drugs in the same breath as "recreational." I'd said I didn't mind working shamanic when I spoke to him on the phone—that might be taken for informed consent of a sort. And Miriam had gone back freely for months—surely she'd known what he was using?

I tried to sell myself on that all the way home and failed. Okay, Ruslan used chemicals in his rituals out of a countercultural sense of giddy irresponsibility—but he'd been very responsible when he set his coven to kill Miriam by magic. He'd said right out that he wanted her dead and had done his best to make her that way.

And she *was* dead. How he'd killed her didn't matter—or, I admitted, *if* he'd killed her. He'd wanted to. He'd tried to. He would have been just as guilty of *malificarum* if Miriam were still alive.

Morality is even more indigestible than ethics. By the time I made it up five flights of stairs

I was sick of the whole thing. I solved the problem that evening by getting drunk on Slivovitz boilermakers.

Never do that.

9

Friday was the kind of day that gives reincarnation a bad name. I mean, who'd want to do something like this *twice*?

I woke up hungover and with a bad case of attitude that it wasn't hard to pinpoint the cause of. Anger. Frustration. I'd turned over a rock and a whole nest of moral culpability was lying there wriggling, and the only thing I could think to do was put the rock back down.

I gave Bellflower an excerpt from my troubles that night.

"I went up and saw the people Miriam was working with on Wednesday."

Belle and I were drinking tea in her kitchen. Belle's kitchen is four feet wide and was painted gas-chamber green sometime in the 1950s. It's furnished in early Gift Of The Garbage Goddess—curbside salvage—and contains a large number of nonworking appliances that the landlord refuses to remove, as well as Washington Heights' only four-quart teapot.

Nobody else was here yet—I'd left work early in addition to arriving late; the weekly paycheck was going to be on the slim side. Belle was eating fried bananas and *raita* from the Indian place that delivers and I was poking at my chicken curry and feeling morose.

"And?" Belle said.

"And," I said, "they are coercive, nonconsensual, and doing drugs—well, chemicals. There's this stuff in the candles that I'm pretty sure is camphor, and stuff in the wine—"

"So why did you go there?" Belle asked in her best voice of sanity. I stared at her.

"To find out what they were doing."

"And now you know. And you won't go back there, right?"

I looked at her. "You're getting at something, aren't you?"

Belle dipped a banana in yogurt. "You told me that they were pretty secretive, didn't you?"

"Yeah." I'd told her just about what Julian had told me, and left out the invitational phone call from Ruslan.

"And so it's not like they were running something open. Probably they let you come to their meeting because you were a friend of Miriam's."

"Yeah. Right. And then they told me they put a deathspell on Miriam for trying to leave the coven."

That finally got Belle's attention. "Are you serious?"

"I swear it by the Goddess, Belle. They had her *athame,* the one I gave her, and they said they killed her because she broke her oath to them."

Belle regarded me critically, although not as though she was about to leap up and go for the police.

"Well, no wonder she called you, if that was the kind of head trip they were putting on her. People like that make me so mad—and that kind of power-tripping, you just *know* it's built on secrecy and disinformation. And it's so stupid—the Craft isn't about coercion and fear, it's about knowledge and empowerment."

"Somebody's empowerment, anyway," I said. I'd pushed one of Belle's buttons and got one of the standard fifteen-second screeds; she does a lot of public-awareness outreach. "It doesn't matter what the Craft's 'about' when somebody's using it for something else."

Belle sighed. "I thought we'd got over this Witch-war stuff. These are the nineties—this mystification and blind-faith Ancient Atlantean Magus stuff doesn't do anybody any good."

"It sure didn't do Miriam any good," I snapped.

Belle got the expression on her face that she gets when she's trying to be open-minded and not say anything to contradict somebody else's value system.

"Look, Bast. We all know about negative magic. There is no excuse for it. It's wrong. But it's out there, and everybody deals with it in their own way. It can't hurt you unless you open yourself to it. You just have to stay grounded in the earth-plane."

The day I discovered that all Witches don't believe in magic was a great shock to me. It was also long enough ago that I was no longer surprised that Belle, who is my friend and I love her, could say in one breath that the Magic Power of Witchcraft could reverse everything from cancer to tooth decay and in the next that black magic can't kill. Personally, I have always believed that the tail goes with the dog.

"Belle, these people are into power-tripping and weirdness and black magic. When somebody tells you they've killed somebody, what do you do?"

The bell for the downstairs door rang and Belle pushed the buzzer to unlock it. When she looked back at me her mind was made up.

"I really don't know what to tell you, Bast. If you're looking for a villain you'll find one, and you could let this take over your life. But Miriam's dead and you're not—and what could you do, anyway? There isn't some central validating agency that decides who's a real Witch and who isn't. Different traditions have different value systems. You can't just stand here and say this is right because I like it and this is wrong because I don't like it, because those are not judgments based on objective criteria."

"Murder?" I suggested.

Belle smiled sadly at me. "Everybody has their own way of dealing with the truth," she said. "How are you going to prove that something Ruslan did magically was the real cause of Miriam's death?"

I couldn't. Because I didn't *know* that Miriam

had died of liver failure, and even if the autopsy proved it, *I* couldn't prove to the satisfaction of the police or anyone else that Ruslan had given her the chloroform that (maybe) caused it.

And Belle was right. Even though he'd confessed to doing something that was wrong by Gardnerian tenets, it was undoubtedly right by Khazar rules—and there was no Neopagan ecclesiastical court to bring him up on charges in front of, anyway.

No temporal authority. No spiritual authority. Nobody with any clout to call Michael Ruslan a bad boy.

Part of me hoped, cravenly, that Ruslan had been well and truly frightened by Miriam's death. That it had been the tonic dose of reality he needed to stop dicking around in his syncretic dreamtime and either grow up or get out of the Community.

Because down at the back of my mind was the knowledge that anyone who isn't a white Protestant Christian from a mainstream denomination is getting his or her religious freedom eroded every time the Supreme Court meets, and a nice big case of witchcraft murder could give all of us—Witches, Neopagans, Goddess-worshipers, and even the Iron Johnnies—more attention from bureaucrats and name-takers than most of us could possibly stand.

Paranoia. Right up Lace's alley. Don't even think of going after Ruslan because it would rock the boat into broad daylight.

My public position had always been that

John Q. Mundane did not give a damn about what the rest of us worshiped as long as we didn't do it on Wall Street and scare the insider traders. And I still thought that. Mostly.

So I wanted Ruslan quietly brought to justice—but I'd settle for him just drying up and blowing away.

As of Friday night, I still believed he might do that.

On Saturdays the Revel opens at noon. I put on my New York blacks and lots of my funkiest jewelry and half a dozen rings and the beaded belt pouch that holds my cards and another one for my keys and subway tokens so I wouldn't have a purse to watch and went.

Everything looked different, and it didn't make me feel any better to know it was just me. Everybody else was the same; just as admirable or as contemptible as they'd ever been. They'd never been saints. They weren't quislings now, no matter what Ruslan had done or thought he'd done.

Maybe I was burnt out. Maybe I should gafiate—Get Away From It All. Take up a quiet life of secularity and stop worrying about questions to which the twentieth century has thrown away the answers in a body; questions like morals and ethics and fault and responsibility. Justice. Restitution.

Revenge.

I actually stopped at a liquor store on the way to the Revel and bought a half-pint of brandy. It was a cheap, obvious, and useless escape, and the eagerness with which I went after it scared me enough to keep me from opening the bottle.

But I'd still bought it.

I got to the Revel about ten-thirty. Tollah saw me and opened up for me.

"Oh, Bast, blessed be! You're a real life-saver—Mischia had to go out to Crown Point for a wedding—her brother—and she thought it was Sunday or next week or something and if it was next week I could've told everybody this week that we weren't doing it next week but you see—"

"Just remember me in your will."

Tollah looked nervous, and for the life of me I couldn't figure out why. I recollected the paper bag I was holding and handed it to her. "Here. Contributions to the community chest."

She saw what was in it and gave me a funny look. I went over and sat down at the table set up in the corner for the Tarot reader.

It was one of those collapsible card tables, and it was draped in a purple pall embroidered with Ur and Geb and Nut and all those Egyptian guys. I'd seen it a dozen times, but this was the first time I'd ever looked at the corner with the signature painstakingly embroidered in genuine J. R. R. Tolkien Elvish. It wasn't too hard to make out the transliteration. Sunshrike.

Miriam.

Damn her anyway. If I'd been her worst enemy she couldn't have done worse by me than opening up this Khazar can of worms in my face.

There were little blue card-outlines embroidered into the cloth in the Celtic Cross pattern, not that I needed the *aide de memoire.* I got out my deck and began to shuffle.

People always ask me if I "believe" in Tarot cards. It's pretty easy to do: I own five decks of them. What they mean, of course, is "Do you believe that Tarot cards can tell the future?" and the answer to that is yes—and no.

You can tell the future. If you wear a white cashmere sweaterdress to an important lunch, there is an eighty percent chance that you will spill shrimp cocktail or something else with tomato sauce on it—if only because you're so worried about spilling something that you go all awkward. You *know* this, but you're unlikely to act on the information, even if your mother, your roommate, and your best friend all tell you so.

But if the cards tell you so—and mind, tell you what you already know—you're more likely to accept and act upon the advice, wear bottle-green wool gabardine, and avoid serious grief and dry-cleaning bills. Tarot is a way of sorting out what's bothering you and getting advice from the best-informed source—you—in a way that you're likely to listen to.

So I lay out your cards and tell you all the things your mind is busy sweeping under the rug so it can get on with its business of complicating your life. As for where *I* get the information—well, go figure. But I'm right more often than I'm wrong.

There is something exciting about working with the cards. The more you work to match your knowledge and skill to the seemingly random spill, to understand this one of the seventy-eight-to-the-thirteenth-power possible combinations of symbols and positions and what it means for the woman sitting opposite you, the more you become conscious of reporting only the high points of a river, and the more you become aware of the unchanging subtext of that river; the eternal dialogue with sundered self. I saw the cards and listened to the river, and that took all my concentration. My own problems lost their importance.

It's a lot like jogging.

My first client of the day came over and sat down. I handed her the cards and watched her shuffle and cut. She had no trouble shuffling seventy-eight outsized cards. Probably she read Tarot herself, but there's the "who shaves the barber" paradox: Tarot readers can't generally read for themselves. You lie to yourself. You might as well watch television.

I didn't ask her what she'd come to find out. That comes later, after you see what the cards say.

She handed me the deck back. As I took them they sprayed out of our hands, cards going everywhere. One of them flipped over. The Chariot.

Or as some people call it, the Fool's Paradise. I scooped the cards all back together and began laying them out.

I try to keep omens in their proper perspective.

Carrie brought me a tofu pita and a soda at about two. Traffic had been brisk; there were still about half a dozen women waiting for readings. Lace was behind the counter, with her hair all hennaed, oiled, and spiked out, looking like dangerous sculpture.

Sometimes, despite all your best shuffling, the same cards will turn up over and over again from reading to reading. This can be interpreted in many ways—from poor manual dexterity skills to the possibility that the people being read for are somehow linked. One of the common interpretations of the phenomenon is that the recurring cards are messages meant for the reader.

I'd been seeing a lot of The Chariot today. A young man crowned in glory, his chariot canopied in stars, rides forth from the walled city he has conquered. You have to look at the card for a few seconds before you see that the animals that pull the chariot have neither reins nor bridles. It's the Captain James T. Kirk card, the card of leaping before looking, of burned bridges and uncovered asses. The card of thinking you know what's going on when you don't.

As a message to the reader, it was ambiguous.

Lace saw me see her and waved: black leather fingerless gloves with spikes across the knuckles. I looked down at my rings and necklaces. We were all in our best identity war paint today, dripping with symbols of being who we wished to seem.

And who was Bast—*Lady* Bast, High Priestess of the Wicca?

"When a man's partner is killed, he's sup-

*posed to do something about it. It doesn't make
any difference what you thought of him. He was
your partner and you're supposed to do something about it."*

But I wasn't Sam Spade. I wasn't even the
Queen of the Witches. Miriam wasn't my partner. And Ruslan hadn't broken any laws.

I took a bite of the pita and opened the soda
and went back to telling other people how the
cards said they should run their lives.

The Chariot. Willful stupidity. Fool's Paradise, as in "Living In A—"

What was I missing? If anything?

And what should I do about it?

About five o'clock I looked up and there
wasn't anybody standing around waiting. I
wrapped up my cards and stuffed them back in
my belt pouch. I stretched, and wiggled my fingers, and stood up, and generally indicated that
the cartomancer was done for the day.

Lace came over and folded up the cloth, and
the card table, and the chairs, and I leaned
against the jewelry case and hung out. The Revel
was open until nine, but sometime sooner than
that some assortment of us would be going out
to dinner, and eventually I was going to have to
talk to Lace.

I still felt as if I'd lost my last pair of rose-
colored glasses. I didn't like it. It meant thinking
about too many things—and if the goal of modern life is satisfaction, ratiocination was taking
me further from it every minute. So life is unfair,
people are amoral jerks, we're all going to die,
and as a race humanity is too stupid to put out

the fire in a burning house. Life is the business of forgetting all that, and the sooner I could get on with life, the better.

I made a good stab at forgetting any number of things at dinner. It was about seven by the time that got underway, what with closing the shop up and everything, and by the time everything had jelled it was Lace, Tollah, me, and three other women who had accrued during the wait. Tollah and Lace knew them and I didn't. We went to a new cheap Thai place a few blocks away and stuffed ourselves on things cooked with coriander and coconut milk. I had several beers, since it was courtesy of the Revel.

Lace kept giving me meaningful looks and I kept willfully ignoring them. If I didn't have to talk about *Baba Yaga,* I didn't have to think about *Baba Yaga.* I knew I was being hard on Lace, but on the other hand, if she knew what I knew, she too would have to sit here deciding between life in prison and impotence. Maybe I was acting out of charity.

Lace nailed me during a lull in the conversation. "You are holding out on me, you damn vanilla bitch."

I glanced around. Tollah had her back to us, talking to the three women. I gathered that they were Dianic Gaians, and I hoped nobody would tell me what that was.

"Will you for gods' sake lighten up? You want me to do my John Barrymore imitation or something?" I sotto voced at her.

John Barrymore was one of the most talented

drunks ever produced by the great Barrymore line, and when he died his friends stole his body from the funeral home and used it to scare the shit out of Errol Flynn. I wondered if I would ever have friends like that. If I did, I hoped I would outlive them.

"You said you'd tell me tonight what happened Wednesday. So it's tonight," Lace insisted.

"I can't do it here," I insisted right back.

Lace grabbed my wrist with a hand that resembled one of those devices you use to shape sheet metal. If I hadn't had my Third Degree bracelet on she would have crippled me.

"You can damn well tell me here if she had a lover!"

There were tears in Lace's eyes, and I realized that all the Khazar Trad meant to her was the people who had taken Miriam away from her. She'd like to think they were rotten, but I didn't think that even Lace's wildest imaginings were wild enough to match the truth I'd uncovered.

I thought I knew what she'd do if she knew what I knew. And what the Real World would do to her. I didn't want that to happen.

"It wasn't like that." Out of the corner of my eye I saw Tollah take an interest in our conversation. "She was leaving them, okay? No lover."

Eventually the party broke up. Lace and I walked Tollah back to the Revel.

"So you want to invite me over to your place for a beer?" I asked, when Tollah was inside.

"Cheap bitch," said Lace, and threw an arm around my shoulders.

* * *

I knew that Lace shared a two-bedroom apartment with three other like-minded women way
up north near Columbia, but I'd never been
there until tonight. Sliced four ways the rent
was bearable—just. Lace and one of the others
had the bedrooms, and the other two shared the
converted dining room.

I would bet good money there isn't a single
dining room in all of New York City being used
actually for dining, outside of a few Park Avenue
atavisms. In Manhattan you spell dining room
"extra bedroom."

"They're out," said Lace comprehensively as
we got inside.

The living room was furnished in that bizarre
accretion of furniture gathered by women who
have always been roommates—i.e., have lived
their lives in a succession of bedrooms in
houses or apartments that they don't themselves rent. A lifestyle like that doesn't run to
couches or coffee tables, and even when where
you're living now has room for one you don't buy
it, because where you're living next might not,
and then you'd have to leave it behind with people you (may) have grown to hate.

The living room of Lace's modern urban com-
mune contained six chairs of wildly differing
ethnology—from overstuffed Conran's uphol-
stered in black polished cotton to a rather nice
Biedermeier rocker—two mismatched book-
cases and a salvage-it-yourself table that had
been painted in gaudy Peewee Herman colors.
There was a fake Tiffany lamp and one in Star

Trek *moderne*. The walls were the same way—it was like living with a multiple personality affective disorder case where all the personalities got equal say in the decoration.

Lace got both of us "lite" American beers from the kitchen. She opened hers, and sat down, and *waited* at me.

"Okay," I said. I'd had all dinner to make up my mind and Lace herself to tell me what tack to take. "Her coven leader called me up last week and invited me to a Circle."

And then I lied. Oh, I got all the facts right—at least the ones I told. But I'd never told Lace about Miriam's magical diaries or my midnight phone calls, and I didn't tell her now.

Nor did I tell her about the poison Ruslan was feeding to his coveners or the fact that he'd boasted of working toward Miriam's death. I didn't tell her how he made my skin crawl, or how on sober reflection I was willing to bet that Starfawn was his next victim; a new wannabe Witch to Trilby-ize. Lace didn't need to know all that. Lace didn't *want* to know all that. Lace wanted to know that Miriam had loved her till she died, and that I could tell her without lying.

"So . . . they were sort of *mondo* weird, and I'm pretty sure that Miriam had gotten fed up with them and that they were trying to scare her into staying when she called me. They're not exactly lily-white magically, if you know what I mean. So when she died . . . I guess she'd talked about me, and they wanted to find out if she'd talked *to* me."

"She wouldn't even talk to *me*," grumbled Lace.

"They have a secrecy riff that makes the Gardnerian oath look like the Freedom of Information Act."

Lace laughed, a little gruffly, and raised her beer can.

"Well, here's to all goddamn dumb femmes and dykes. Screw 'em all."

Which seemed, as an epitaph, good enough for anyone, really.

10

Lace invited me to stay the night. It wasn't even a pass, really, but I turned it down all the same. I wanted to go home and pull my covers up over my head and sleep forever or at least until Sunday afternoon, and maybe when I woke up I'd be my old cheerful self again. I had a doom-laden feeling, as if I'd forgotten something terribly important, and I could not imagine what it was.

I found out.

There was no way I could have mundanely known what was waiting for me five flights up when I walked into my home lobby. I told myself stories of imaginary muggers lying in wait in the doorway, but there weren't any. I assured myself that all my neighbors had been smoking crack and fighting, which accounted for the vibes in the air, but that wasn't it either.

My apartment's down the end of a hall, and of

course the hallway lights don't work. I stepped in the blood before I saw it.

In New York the apartment doors are metal. Someone had thoughtfully affixed a wooden board to mine. It looked as if something might be painted on it, but I couldn't be sure, because somebody had also nailed a cat to the board, and then cut the cat open and nailed its ribs to the board, and then stuck everything that was left inside full of razors.

I thought I saw it move, but it couldn't have. It could *not* have—it had been dead for hours and most of the blood on the floor was dry.

I backed up. And then I was sure that was a dreadful mistake, too, because I felt my back hair prickle the way it does when there's someone behind you.

But there wasn't. The hall was empty, yet full of presence, and I had the conviction that the moment I'd taken my eyes off it the cat had begun to pull itself free from the board, and once it was free it would come for me, full of razors.

I looked back at it quickly. Had it moved? Had they done that to it while it was *still alive?*

There were big nails through the eye sockets, holding the head to the board.

"I'll put your eyes out, Witch-bitch." I heard the words from the phone call I'd gotten the day after Miriam died as clearly as if someone was saying them now. *Baba Yaga.*

Reason told me there was no threat, only horror, in the hallway. Intuition assured me the danger was urgent.

I could not enter my apartment any more than I could have done that to an animal—alive or dead—myself. But someone had done it. And they meant to do it to me. The sense of someone in the hallway with me was strong, and none of the mind-tricks I knew would make it go away.

But I could make myself go away. I pulled in my perception, my imagination, my intellect—all the things your mind can use against you. I would not think, I would not feel, I would not imagine. When all of that was gone I forced myself back down the stairs.

I got to the lobby, and instead of going out the front I went down another half-flight and went out the back. There's a sort of a courtyard and a long roofed alleyway leading to the street behind. I went down it without hesitation, even though it was pitch dark. Then I was out on the street again, feeling things swirling around inside me like the demons in Pandora's box and over everything the raw sense of someone—some*thing*—that had been cheated.

I wanted to go back up those stairs. I wanted it desperately. I could see myself unlocking the door and going inside. I tried to see myself locking the door again and making myself safe, but I couldn't bring that image into focus. I'd go in, and leave the door unlocked behind me. Then I'd drink—I wanted a drink; I'd been drinking beer all evening and I wanted something to keep me from sobering up.

And anyone who wanted could come up the stairs and get at me. Anyone who knew I was there to find. Anyone who'd made sure I'd be there.

I was cold sober now. And I wasn't going back. I pushed back against the insistent images, not letting myself feed them. I was a Child of the Goddess; if the Wicca was for anything, it was for a time like this. I was the Goddess, and She was me, and into that charmed circle of light no blackness could penetrate.

I reached Broadway and flagged a cab. I didn't dare take the subway. There was too much *possibility* in the subway.

It was July first, and eighty-five degrees at 1:30 A.M. My teeth were chattering uncontrollably.

One of Lace's roommates let me in. I'd banged on the door until somebody answered, and when she finally took the chains off the door and opened it I barged in past her like she was furniture. Everybody was up by then; when Lace saw me she just put her arms around me.

I must have looked like a rape victim. The other two kept asking if I could identify . . . someone. My perceptions jump-cut with the discontinuity of shock; one minute one of them would be there, and when I tried to answer she'd be gone, coming back with tea or brandy or a wet washcloth.

It was a reaction way out of proportion to that common urban inconvenience of coming home and finding a dead cat nailed to your door. But it was perfectly in line with a reaction to a murder attempt. Because that was what it had been.

A deathspell for a Witch.

One of the charming old European folk customs thankfully not perpetuated in the Community at large today is that of taking a sheep or pig's heart and pricking it full of pins, nails, glass, and anything similar you might have lying about—like razor blades. This is guaranteed to be certain death for the Witches in your neighborhood—once you've got the thing ready, you take it and bury it under the doorstoop of the Witch you most particularly dislike.

They'd nailed it to mine. *Baba Yaga.*

I'd been innocent beyond permission to think Ruslan didn't know exactly who I was. He'd known about Changing's Crossing Circle. He'd known enough to call me and try to stop it. Yet when I went to his circle, not one comment about Changing or my Craft affiliations. I'd assumed he didn't know.

Now I knew better. He knew. He just didn't care. He'd had me out to Queens to look me over, and like a mindless sacrificial goat I'd gone. Now he'd made up his mind what to do, and he was doing it. I was not even bothering to be fair and open-minded and pretend that somebody else in little old New York might be trotting out the old *malificarum* to torture cats to death and nail them to my door. There wasn't anybody else.

Just Ruslan—and his Khazar coven that had gotten a taste for blood, murder, and vendetta, and wanted the thrill of hunting down another victim, even if they had to manufacture one themselves.

Eventually I looked around the Real World.

The others had gone; it was just Lace and me, and she was holding my hands. Eventually I realized I was the one holding her hands, and let go.

"I didn't tell you quite everything about *Baba Yaga*," I said. My throat ached as if I'd been screaming.

I guess I was lucky; if I'd been in any better shape Lace would've decked me sure. As it was, she heard me out and put me to bed.

I'd been wrong about Lace. Vendettas weren't her style. She accepted absolutely the idea that Ruslan had murdered Miriam, no question, but she also accepted that there was nothing she could do about it. The great Anti-Pagan and Lesbian Conspiracy would ensure that justice could not be done. She was bitter, but fatalistic.

She also loaned me the money later that day to go shopping for what I needed and then came back with me to my apartment, on a bright and reasonably sunny morning in the later twentieth century when the idea of worshiping gods was as unbelievable as the concept that someone would try to kill someone else with magic.

The *thing* was still on the door. In the morning sunlight with Lace at my back it was gross but not terrifying, all its potential for harm leached away.

Maybe.

Lace and I levered the board off the door and slid it into the garbage bag we'd brought, and poured a mixture of Lysol and Uncrossing Floorwash over the door and the floor and mopped everything up with paper towels until my end of the hall was cleaner than it had been in years. I couldn't get the residue of the carpet tape used to mount the board off the door, but I guessed I was going to have to settle. Only when everything was neat and tidy and I'd blessed the whole door frame with patchouli and blue chalk did I unlock my door.

Everything inside was serene. The sun illuminated a solid bar of dust motes on its way to the sink. I felt like I'd gotten a stay of execution.

"Tea?" I said to Lace.

"Beer," said Lace firmly. She picked up the bag full of dead cat and bloody paper towels. "You want I should toss this for you?"

"No," I said. It went against all of my training and self-preservation instincts to just throw a major spell-component out with the trash to go on wreaking havoc, but I would not take it into the apartment to give it a really good psychic eradication. "We can't just leave something like that lying around ungrounded."

So I brought newspapers and tape and a box out into the hall and wrapped what had been on my door in a nice neat package. Later that day I dropped it off at a place that accepts UPS packages even on Sunday.

I came back from that alone and let myself in to my apartment again. This time it was evening, and the place had the overbaked scent of someplace that had been shut up for a whole summer's day. I wished Ruslan much joy of his package when he opened it, one to four days from now.

Miriam's little Goddess of the Games glimmered down at me from her place on my altar. I smiled up at her and lit some incense and paused, like a mirror, for reflection.

I had been the victim of a magical attack.

Credulity stretched. Oh, they were a major topic of conversation among newbies and wannabes at Pagan festivals. Everyone was almost certain they'd been the victim of one. It was a good explanation for everything from a case of herpes to being fired, and so flattering to be the center of attention of an emissary from the Unseen World. Even I, once and a long time ago, had Almost Certainly created a magical child that haunted me for some weeks knocking books off shelves until I got bored with it.

Eventually you grow up, find out how the laws of magic actually work, and stop making an ass of yourself in public. Because real gen-u-wine ducks-in-a-row Black Workings are just about as rare as actual persecution of Witches. Rarer.

But not, I'd just found out, nonexistent.

I could not walk away from this now. I could not wring my hands and say that I could not build a temporal case, and so no spiritual measures need be taken. Not anymore.

I'd been given the chance, on which I'd rather have took a miss, of gazing on the naked face of capital-E Evil, the thing which, as Hannah Arendt more or less says, does things just because it can. And I could not do nothing.

Caring is what separates good from evil, not the motions you make with your body. A lot of the motions are identical in the gray area that the moderns say proves that there is neither Good nor Evil. Dion Fortune said that Evil is only misapplied Good, which was a brave thing to say in the time where she was living, but she never lived to see the worst aftermath of the War To End War.

If we have a soul, a better nature, any altruism at all, Evil is its autism. Evil is Evil, proving that even tautologies can be true.

And now I had to do something about it, without doing something Evil myself, because if I looked at it and called it by its True Name and then walked away, it had me. You aren't born with a soul. You purchase it in installments. And I'd just been handed the bill for the next one.

Hubris. What a lovely convenient thing a label is. Better than a straitjacket for pulling all your energy into fighting it.

Ruslan was doing evil. Ruslan had to be stopped. But he had committed no provable crime against the people of the City and State of New York. And there was no central authority in the Community that could or would stop him.

I was the only one who knew the truth.

Heady stuff, that. Bast, Lone Ranger of the Wicca. A free ride to megalomaniac paranoia.

Truth, we are taught, does not come from consensus, but from knowledge. The knowledge was there, but somehow I didn't think Ruslan would hold still while I trotted a jury of his peers past his questionable ethical practices.

And even if everyone in the Community believed me, what would they do? Anything?

Ha. I'd already heard Belle's vote. "We are not qualified to sit in judgment. . . ."

Yet I could not do nothing. And that was the bone in the throat—I had to do something. Something legal, and more to the point, moral.

I curled up in a chair where I could see Miriam's little Goddess, pulled out one of my sketchbooks, and began to think.

It took me a week to get what I wanted, but most of that was because the typesetter was so damn slow—closed for the Fourth, and other light holidays. During that period Ruslan was blessedly silent, package or no.

Lace phoned me a couple of times, but we didn't have much to say to each other. I hung out around the Revel a bit, but I really didn't fit into their feminism-and-granola Paganism any more than I did with the Serpent's Truth's heavy-metal high sorcery.

Where did I belong? My own High Priestess thought I was overreacting, and Belle was pretty much middle-of-the-road as Witches went. If I didn't belong in Wicca, what was left?

I wouldn't worry about that now. I belonged to the Goddess at least—that's one good thing about *gnosis*. And I thought that what I was doing was right.

And whether it was right or not, it was still what I was doing.

I picked up the type Friday noon, and stayed late at the studio mechanicaling it up. When I was done it was a poster—a handbill, really—8½ × 11, easy to reproduce at any city copy shop, full of big black letters.

WARNING: There is a Black Coven operating out of Queens. They call themselves Baba Yaga and claim to practice a Khazar (Russian) Wiccan tradition. These people perform black magick and use dangerous (illegal) drugs in their rituals without the consent of the participants. They have already been responsible for the death of one woman who was trying to leave them. If you were a friend of or knew Sunshrike, avoid these people and warn your friends.

The wording had been what took me the most time to get right. I hadn't mentioned Ruslan's name, or added my own to the poster. I had tried to make it something that would have no effect in the mundane world—I could not imagine these posters causing Ruslan to lose his Real World job or make the police come looking for him. All I wanted was to neutralize Ruslan in the same arena where he and *Baba Yaga* were trying to kill me, not to raise the stakes.

And that is the difference between Good and Evil, and the reason Good never wins.

That night I took the mechanical home and cast a spell of my own—an intention, really—that the poster it made should shine such a bright light that the shadows people needed to

work evil would no longer exist. The next day—
Saturday—I took it to the Eighth Street Copy
Shop and ordered twenty-five hundred copies.

Saturday night at 8:30 I went down to the Revel,
hoping Lace was there. In spite of the weather
(hot but clear) I was wearing an extra-extra-
large army surplus parka, which I keep for wearing to Pagan Festivals because nothing in its sad
shabby life is ever going to make any difference
to it again. I had reinforced its immense pockets
with duct tape; they contained fifteen-hundred
flyers, a staple gun and two boxes of staples, and
a dozen glue sticks. I looked like a mugger waiting to happen.

I waddled into the store. Mischia, having got
her brother safely married, was sitting behind
the card table finishing up a late customer. A
coffee can full of bills sat at her elbow. Lace
looked up from the cash register. The henna was
black now, and so were her fingernails. She
looked like a punk vampire whose mother'd had
a heavy date with a Mack truck.

"Hi, Lace—doing anything tonight?" I said in
my best Donna Reed voice.

"Keeping you out of Bellevue, maybe. Shit,
Bast, what's with you?"

I went over to where Mischia wouldn't hear
us. "I just joined the Occult Police," I told Lace.

"I'm telling you because I figured you'd guess."

It was an hour later; we were outside the
Revel and Tollah was locking up inside. She
hadn't raised an eyebrow over the arctic parka

in July. I wondered how strange people thought I was.

I handed Lace a flyer. It was hard to stand there while she read it and wait for her to laugh. I was doing this because I *had* to; the same way you have to move your hand out of a candle flame. I didn't think she'd agree with me.

"And you're going to put these up all over town?" Lace said, poker-faced.

"You will have noticed my name's not on them."

"Yeah, sure. That's really going to confuse the hell out of people, Bast."

"But they can't prove anything. Just like I can't prove that *Baba Yaga* poisoned Miriam and nailed a cat to my door."

Lace laughed then. Maybe the irony of it amused her, or maybe she was just tickled at the thought that I was never going to laugh at her Conspiracy paranoia again.

"Sure. Okay. Where do we start?"

If you take a map of New York and turn it so that Battery Park is at the bottom and Spuyten Duyvil is at the top (the name has nothing to do with the devil; it's Dutch for *whirlpool*), Chanter's Revel is the occult shop nearest the bottom. So we started there and worked our way uptown.

I stapled flyers to fences and glued them to lampposts. I slid them through the mail slots of the stores we visited. I hit up bookstores, bars, *botanicas*, and any other likely looking funky New Age place I saw. I think there are "Post No Bills" regulations still on the books in Manhattan; Lace kept lookout and we were careful to make sure nobody saw me actually doing anything. It was a clear night; eventually Goddess Luna made it up over the buildings to shine down on the Batman and Robin of the Neopagan Community.

I glued several flyers to the windows of The Snake. I didn't do that anywhere else, because glue stick is hell to remove and I had no grudge against the owners of the walls I was decorating, but I suspected Julian of knowing more about Ruslan than he'd told me. Petty, I know.

When I'd done a street, I could look back down and see my handbills: lemon yellow, orange orange, and raspberry red. The fluorescent copier paper had cost extra, but it'd been well worth it. Nobody could miss them.

Eventually we ran out. I had another thousand at home, and the original, so I could make more any time I wanted to, but what I'd been carrying had pretty well plastered the Village. The only occult shop I'd missed was Mirror Mirror, which is pretty chichi and New Age—and way over on the West Side, besides.

The full moon was sliding off toward the east—that made it a little after midnight. I felt an incredible sense of euphoria; whether it was the presence of the Goddess or the rush that comes from making mischief, I didn't bother to examine.

"Buy you a midnight snack?" I said to Lace. "I figure you owe me, Caped Crusader."

* * *

I avoided my usual haunts on Sunday, so as not to be seen too obviously smirking. The sense of well-being I'd lucked into on Saturday continued; it's wonderful to bask in approval, even if it's only yours.

I coasted uptown and spent the day window-shopping on the Upper East Side and thinking that if I got my hands on enough of the right pieces of Art Nouveau I could convince Neopagans everywhere that the Victorians were a Goddess-worshiping matriarchy. I entertained once more the unlikely dream of Owning My Own Occult Shop, which I never will because more than fifty percent of all businesses go bankrupt in the first year and I'm too smart to get into things with a failure factor that high.

I tell myself.

I splurged on a sushi dinner—one last time, since with taxis and cleaning supplies and all (not to mention the book I'd bought at The Snake in the middle of all this) I was going to have to put in serious hours at the Bookie Joint to stay on the profits side of the ledger. But that gnawing feeling of being a helpless consentor to what *Baba Yaga* had done to Miriam was gone.

I felt up enough to make a pass by Cindy's on the way home, but the salon had closed up shop. I saw a couple of my posters on the buildings nearby. They looked like I felt. Cheery.

My answering machine was taking a message as I walked in. Belle wanted me to call her. She'd wanted me to call her, I found, at eleven, one, and three P.M. also.

And her all the way up at the top of the is-

land, and this such a secret between us. I tried
to wipe the smirk off my face and failed.

There was also a message from Lace to tell me
she'd gotten Tollah to post a copy of the flyer
inside the shop. I looked at the pile I had left.
Maybe she'd like some to hand out, too.

You would think that Martin Luther had never nailed ninety-five theses to anything—or that there weren't handbills all over the city telling people everything from the date of the Apocalypse to the Queen of England's sexual habits. Why should they make such a fuss about one more?

Belle nailed me at the studio Monday.

"Bast? I really think we ought to talk about this," she said as soon as I picked up the phone.

"I'm not really somewhere I can talk," I said, not even bothering to deny I knew what "this" was.

I was safe because it was true: Ray doesn't object to my religion (if he's noticed it), but he does object to tying up Houston Graphics' one phone line for anything other than Houston Graphics business.

"I had no idea you were so upset about Miriam," she said. "I know you can't talk now, but will you come over tonight? I really feel bad about not having been more there for you."

"If I can," I hedged. "Look, I'll call you later."

But I didn't go to Belle's later. I went down to The Snake.

The Snake opens every day at noon and remains open until ten or midnight, depending on the will of Tris, Julian, and the gods. When I got there around seven, the usual house-party atmosphere prevailed. There were leather boys with rosy crosses tattooed on their pecs hobnobbing with *brujas* wearing every piece of jewelry known to medical science and enough mascara to equip a Tammy Faye Bakker impersonator. There were people for whom the sixties hadn't ended and those who were already living in the Age of Horus. It was pure sleaze. I felt instantly at home and wondered why.

There was a copy of my flyer on the bulletin board, and I definitely hadn't put it there. Lace hadn't either—she'll cross the threshold of The Snake about the same time she goes into St. Pat's. I slithered past the bulletin board and down one of the aisles, where I picked up a book by a Brit anthropologist who got herself inducted into an English coven. She concluded that belief in magic causes belief in magic, provided the believer wants to believe.

Well, hell, *I* knew that. Belief is what makes it work. In theory unbelief should work the same way, but the mind is a divided camp at the best of times. You can eradicate reason from your mind much easier than you can banish superstition. In the end, the reality of magic has to be decided by each person for himself, with full knowledge of the consequences.

Magical theory has never been popular with the masses.

I worked my way around past Atlantis and the Rosicrucians to the front desk. Julian was behind the cash register, presiding over his little kingdom. When he saw me he blinked, as if he couldn't believe his eyes.

"Bast—I was hoping you'd come by."

Not convincing. And Julian was always convincing. Right then little warning bells started to go off in my head.

"You've got a book for me, Julian?" What was it really? He couldn't be picking this inopportune a time to discover an interest in girls.

I was standing between the bulletin board and the cash register; behind me two gays were discussing the Baba Yaga flyer in the patented New York Gay Male Accent.

"Remember how a couple weeks ago you were in with that Russian thing?" Julian said, ignoring what I'd just said. Behind me the conversation turned on the imperialistic judgmentalism of whoever had prepared the flyer. "Do you still have it?"

That was the moment at which I knew what I hadn't even suspected, but I shoved the knowledge down in order to concentrate on what I was saying. I tried desperately to remember what I'd told Julian about the Khazar missal. "Maybe," I said.

"Burn it," Julian said flatly.

I stared at him, looking like a moron and for once not even caring. Because I'd been right when I pasted all those flyers on The Snake's windows—Julian *did* know more than he was telling.

Julian was the one who'd sold me out to Ruslan.

What was the sum total of my relationship with Julian? Charge slips. And what was on those charge slips? Nothing much: just my (mundane) name, address, and phone number. And Julian knew me as Bast.

Julian was the link.

I opened my mouth to say something, but then someone came up to the register and Julian turned away as if he'd never spoken.

"Oh, hey, *Jadis!*" I turned around and stared straight at Starfawn.

Know that your sins will find you out an astute student of human nature said once. Starfawn was standing right in front of the sign and could hardly fail to notice it—assuming she could read.

"It's so neat to see you again. I guess you're feeling okay?" She was good, but she couldn't quite suppress her smirk when she said that. Starfawn of *Baba Yaga* had every reason to hope I wasn't feeling okay.

"I was hoping you'd maybe come back, 'cause you left so fast the last time I really didn't get a chance to talk to you, but Rus said he hadn't heard from you." Her eyes were flat and innocent and brown, completely untroubled. I revised my opinion. Not a Trilby. A little lamprey, hungry for blood.

She looked up at my flyer and dismissed it with a shrug of one bare shoulder. "Somebody's in real trouble for that—but hey, whoever isn't for us is against us, you know?"

I'd heard that somewhere before. Maybe Starfawn thought it was original.

"Who do you suppose could have done something like that?" I said with an increasing sense of unreality.

She smiled; a blinding set of full dental caps. "Well, you know, Bast, honey, Rus is going to find out."

She sashayed right out the door before I realized she'd called me by name. I looked at Julian. He was staring down at me with the blank expression usually worn by the better class of Puritan Witch-burners.

"Bye," he said.

I spent the rest of the evening bludgeoning my feelings about Julian into something I could live with. Every time I started to rationalize his involvement I couldn't decide whether I was being transactional and open-minded or selling out for a pretty face.

He'd given Ruslan my legal name and unlisted phone number. Good guess: He was the only one who could make the connection between Karen and Bast who also might know Ruslan.

On the other hand, he'd advised me to burn the missal. Unsolicited advice, and one of the very few non-mercantile-based conversations I'd ever had with Julian.

Did that mean he repented his wicked ways and thought I was cute, or just that he was playing both ends against the middle to achieve balance, like a good Ceremonial Magician?

By the time I woke up Tuesday morning I decided it probably didn't matter.

But I resolved to make future transactions at The Snake cash only.

Of course the (rumored) authorship of the "Trumpet's Blast Against the Monstrous Regiment of Khazar Wiccans" (to coin a title) didn't stay a secret. For one thing, I had to talk to Belle eventually, even though she had to come all the way down to my apartment to catch me. She asked me point-blank if I'd done it, and then I got a long lecture on tolerance, responsibility, understanding, and Not Making Waves.

She kept reminding me that I didn't have any proof Ruslan was involved in Miriam's death—a confession was apparently no more proof than it would have been in a mundane criminal case.

I hadn't mentioned the cat. I think I was afraid of what I'd do if I did and heard what I thought I would.

"You really don't have any right to go publicizing something like that in that fashion. It isn't constructive, you know, and we all have to tolerate each other, not condemn. If you want to invite Ruslan to a Circle in order to talk things over . . ."

"I am going to Circle with that sonovabitch

motherfuck about the time hell freezes over," I interrupted. "Are you listening to me, Belle? Are you listening to *yourself?* For ten years you've told me that magic works—changes in environment in conformation with will, remember? Well, I believed you, and now when I tell you that there is someone out there using his will like an AK-47, you tell me I'm not being constructive! If it works, it can kill—and that's against all the ethics you taught me, too! Ethics, Belle! Ruslan used black magic against Miriam—he used it against me—he admitted it—"

"Oh, Bast, I think you're taking things way out of context," Belle said, exasperated.

I took a deep breath. "All I want to know is, do you believe all this stuff about ethics and love and magic that you've been pushing at me all these years, or are you just another fucking mundane?"

"I don't think you're being terribly reasonable about this," Belle said in a tight little voice.

"I don't think I'm *going* to be reasonable about this," I said, which pretty well killed that conversation. I didn't offer to walk her to the subway when she left.

Some of the other members of Changing called too, once they'd seen the flyer and heard my name attached to it. The Cat took it as a personal affront that I'd used print media instead of an electronic BBS. Glitter thought I should have hired some of her clients to beat Ruslan up. Everyone was bewildered at my introduction of a real toad into their imaginary garden.

Okay, so magic-with-a-*K* is a crock of shit. Mental masturbation for the masses. Self-delusion. This is not the point. The point is that Ruslan, under the guise of practicing Wicca, violated a number of its central tenets—the Rules. No more enforceable or admirable than the rules in a game of Monopoly, if you like, but start breaking them and soon what you've got left isn't any kind of game at all.

Whether Ruslan was more than a little responsible for the real live death of an actual human being probably doesn't matter either. He'd *tried* to be. And unless my flyer drove him out of the Community, he was going to go on being responsible, until he made a big enough mess to interest the temporal authorities, because nobody in the Community was going to say a word against him.

A central regulating authority is not the answer. There have always been con men and charlatans in the religion business, bilking their followers to build their Towers of Power and their Crystal Cathedrals. There always will be. The only answer is to eliminate followers, but it's lonely when you don't follow the herd.

Maybe there isn't any answer.

Changing's first July meeting was on Friday the 13th. I didn't go. I had my own ritual to conduct.

I'd snagged a nice sturdy box from a trash heap and covered it with wrapping paper. Now I dumped in some potpourri and frankincense and a protection amulet or two, a procedure that always reminds me vaguely of kindergarten arts and crafts time, although I've managed to come to terms with it. And when I had the box looking pretty and inviting and strong in a way that made sense to my unconscious mind, I dumped in all that was left in the world of Miriam Seabrook, including the tapes of the phone messages I'd had from her and Ruslan. Eventually someone would be having a bonfire somewhere and I could burn the lot.

I hesitated a long time over the Khazar missal. Burn it, Julian had said—and while a part of me thought that was a good idea, and something I could manage right now, I couldn't quite bring myself to do it. So I wrapped it in red silk and tucked it into the box along with all the rest.

Then it was all hidden away under my bed. Over and done with, I thought. All that was left was for me to try and make sense of what had happened.

I'd managed to construct a sort of timetable. Sometime in March of this year: Miriam meets Ruslan and joins *Baba Yaga*, taking their oaths of secrecy. At first she's pleased with it. She drops old friends and separates the ones she can't drop completely (like Lace) from her new friends. She starts making her very own Khazar missal, and Ruslan paints her portrait into the icon inside the front cover—with her own blood—just as he has for every new Khazar.

But then things go sour. Maybe it's common sense asserting itself. Maybe the things they're asking her to do finally outweigh the sense of being part of a glorious conspiracy. At any rate, sometime around the beginning of June she tells them she's through with them—or maybe just hints that she's dissatisfied. And Ruslan tells her "once in, never out." He has her *athame*. He tells the coven to do a deathspell. Maybe he tells Miriam. Maybe he doesn't. But Miriam, very conveniently, dies.

I didn't know Ruslan well enough to know if he expected his magic to work. Whether he got what he expected or not, the results frightened him—especially when he realized that Miriam had died with all her Khazar material in her possession.

Miriam's missal was the thing that bound her into *Baba Yaga*. Maybe it was an occult funnel, like Julian said. Or maybe Ruslan only thought it was. But the thought of losing control over it made Ruslan crazy enough to commit an actual crime: tossing Miriam's apartment to look for it. He probably didn't have to break in— Ruslan struck me as the kind of power-tripper who ended up with keys to his coveners' apartments.

Was that how he'd gotten Miriam's *athame*? Or had he made her give it to him? I couldn't imagine her doing that—but I could imagine her fear on coming home and finding it gone. Was that the thing that had finally made her call me?

I'd never know.

But I did know that three days after he trashed her apartment Ruslan phoned me to invite me over to his place. Miriam might have mentioned me—or Julian might have told him I'd showed up at The Snake brandishing the missal. I tried to imagine Julian as a member of

Baba Yaga and failed, fortunately for my sense of *amour propre*. No matter how much ceremony Baba Yaga layered on, they'd still be too Pagan for him.

Which was beside the point. The point was Ruslan, and his telephone soliciting of Yours Truly, part-time moron. Ruslan was still looking for the missal and hoped I had it—in fact, he'd made some pretty heavy-handed threats about what would happen to me if I didn't hand it over. But I didn't, and so, not having gotten it, he summoned up *Baba Yaga* to . . .

Kill me? Scare me? Search my apartment? Make me go running back to him with it clutched in my hot little hand, begging him to make the bogeyman go away?

I didn't know. And I hadn't done any of those things, which was more to the point. Instead, I'd turned the full glare of Community attention on him and made him the current hot topic of gossip. A sensible person would pull in his horns and walk away, but I wasn't sure if Ruslan was one.

And the worst of it was, Ruslan might not be sure either.

12

New York headed into the depths of July. Not as bad as August, when the streets melt, but enough to make me wish I had the money and the organization to afford an air conditioner at home.

Nothing happened.

Oh, I could feel Belle's hurt feelings from one hundred and ninety blocks away, and I spent a serious amount of ritual time making sure my "personal space" was magically clean. Ruslan and I believed in magic, even if the rest of the world didn't.

Some people bootlegged the flyer. I saw some copies I hadn't made in places I hadn't put them. I'd used up the rest of mine strewing them around the city in places you wouldn't normally expect to see things like that, like Rockefeller Center.

But the consensus (or the general consensus of opinion, as our semiliterate friends on the telly would have it) was "judge not, lest ye be judged"—a homily that had never slowed the Christians down any.

And I was perfectly willing to let the gods judge me. It was my peers that bothered me.

Friday night. Coincidentally the twenty-something-th anniversary of the Apollo 11 landing, which had had no effect on life as we know it. Lace had called to invite me special to the Revel's TGIF circle. I was doing the politic thing and staying home. I did not want to be patron saint of the first annual anti-masculinist Dianic Wicca *jihad.* Down at the Revel they'd taken the anti-Khazar manifesto to heart; Ruslan was a perfect *bête noir* for them, being a male Ceremonial Magician who had caused the death of a (sort of) lesbian while practicing god-centered Neopaganism.

I'd seen this before, with the scapegoat of the moment. They'd blow him up to mythic proportions, then get tired of their game and wander off, leaving behind a certified Craft legend.

Nor did I want to replace Miriam in Lace's affections. We'd developed the pressure-cooked emotional bond that comes from being victims of the same trauma, and it was probably better for both of us if natural attrition took its course. In addition to any number of other good reasons for becoming polite strangers again, I wouldn't make Lace any happier than Miriam had.

I was actually considering calling Rachel Seabrook to see if she'd ever gotten any autopsy reports when the phone rang.

"Jello?" I chirped.

"This is Ruslan."

There are times when your power of improvisation deserts you. For some reason I'd never expected to hear from him again. I didn't have a script ready.

"I suppose you think you're very clever," he said, in the tone that daddies everywhere use to begin the scold of the erring nymphet. That saved me; I've never been any daddy's girl and I'm way too old for nymphethood.

"Hello, Michael, it's nice to hear from you." Hearing his first name stopped him for a minute; I'd hoped it would.

"I don't think you'll think so when you hear what I have to say, Karen. I'm calling on the advice of my lawyer about those flyers of yours. You didn't think I knew about them, did you?"

Why not? Aside from their being the hot topic of the last two weeks, I'd even posted some on the Double-R line. He'd probably ridden to work in the same car with them.

"My lawyer thinks he can make a pretty good case for libel, here, but I'm not a vindictive man. If you'll just make some good-faith reparations—"

"What exactly is it that you want?" The song and dance about the lawyer was bullshit; if he had one he wouldn't be talking to me now.

"Look, I know you're kind of overwrought. You know what I mean. But I think I can cut you a little slack. Just give me back the stuff you stole from Miriam's apartment and we can both just walk away."

Oh, he was cool. Nothing I said was going to jar him loose from his preplanned script.

"You know, *Jadis*, a lot worse things than lawyers could happen if you don't. I warned you. The gods of the Khazar are real, and they are not mocked."

"I think that the Khazar gods are getting a little too much help these days," I said. It was pure inspiration, in the literal sense; I had the same feeling of right and proper action I'd had when I posted all those flyers.

"Did you know they're autopsying Miriam Seabrook? Suspicious accidental death. You should have used Mogen David in your fucking Dixie cup, Mikey. There's somebody down in the Manhattan County Coroner's office slicing her liver up with a microtome right now—and when they're done they're going to find your signature all over it. Murder. Plain real-world murder that even the mundanes can believe in."

"Bullshit," said Ruslan.

I laughed. "I've got Miriam's Khazar book and a nice long letter full of names and addresses. Do I have to prove anything—or do they just have to look?"

"Miriam Seabrook died of heart failure!" Ruslan said. *"Baba Yaga—"*

"Ever hear of chemical footprints, jerkball? The traces a drug leaves in the user's body? What's in the wine, Mikey? Something good?"

There was a pause, and the next time he spoke I had difficulty recognizing it as the same voice.

"You cowan *bitch. I am going to bury you."*

The bottom dropped out of reality and I clutched the phone. My heart was hammering as if I'd stared into the open throat of a Hell I professed not to believe in.

I'd gotten his attention, all right. I'd finally made him mad.

I stood there wondering if I dared to hang up, knowing he knew where I lived. Then he laughed. It was a friendly, confident sound that wasn't quite sane anymore.

"You know, you really do have some things that belong to me, Karen. Why don't you give them back?"

You always read in these spatterpunk effusions about terror on top of terror, and despite the bouncing heads and flying entrails, the fear never seems plausible. Maybe you can't get down on paper or film about how *real* terror is what you do to yourself with the knowledge of what the other person can do, and probably will do, when there is nothing at all that you can do to affect his actions.

Why don't you give them back? Because if you don't, some night you'll wake up and I'll be standing there, and I will do things to you that you don't even want to begin to imagine.

If I didn't give Miriam's things to him he'd be mad. Bottom line.

"I'll trade you. Then we're quits." I am not brave, and I wasn't then. It was an atavistic certainty that running from the nightmare would only make it attack that made me say it—that, and the hunch that somewhere on this path lay the only way out.

"*You* want something from *us?* Well, this is unusual." Oh yes, he was willing to string this out now. His *daimon* was riding him, just as mine was me.

"Miriam's *athame*. For the Khazar prayer book."

"I'll be right over."

"It isn't here," I said with quick desperation. Ruslan laughed. "Be reasonable—it's packed up and hidden to mail to the cops—why would I keep it here?—if I died, nobody'd find it."

"You'd be surprised. You know, I don't think you know as much about magic as you claim to, Karen."

"I know I have your book." I wanted to boast about the counterspells I could cast on it, the banishings I could do to make it only a decorated piece of board. But I didn't.

"And you're going to give it to me. And your letter." Perversely, the fact that he believed in that made me feel better. Ruslan of *Baba Yaga* was not omnipotent.

"Tomorrow night. Nine-thirty. St. Mark's Place. Bring Miriam's *athame*. I'll trade you."

"Aren't you going to ask me to come alone?" Ruslan sounded amused. In control.

I hung up on him.

Now I had one more definite fact: Even while he was deluding and drugging his coveners, Ruslan believed what he was telling them. He believed there was magic in the Khazar icons he painted, and the more he failed to get Miriam's back, the more important it became to him, until it became an obsession.

An obsession that I'd played right up to by telling him that the Khazar book could tie him into a murder investigation.

Arguably the stupidest thing I'd ever done.

About an hour later, when I stopped shaking, I realized what had been in the back of my mind when I'd done it. There was no Seabrook murder case. There might not even be an autopsy; New York's a busy town.

But even at nine P.M. there would be people all over St. Mark's Place when I met Ruslan. If I wanted to see some justice done, I had to make a civil pothook on which the temporal courts could hang him.

Frame him? Not quite. I'd just given Ruslan a real good motive to shut me up. It shouldn't be all that hard to get him to assault me. And then I could swear a charge out against him.

If the Goddess was on my side, if magic was afoot in the world, if this was a good idea . . .

If it wasn't, I could just spend the rest of my life looking over my shoulder.

I needed witnesses.

"Hello, Glitter? This is Bast. I need you to do something for me."

Glitter had been one of my partisans during the late unpleasantness with Changing. She was sorry I'd missed coven, glad to hear from me, eager to think everything was going to be fine now. I felt a little guilty drafting her for the role of Sancho Panza. I could have gotten Lace much more easily, but I could never have gotten her to testify afterward.

But Glitter was not only a Probation Officer for the City of New York, she was perfectly willing to come down to St. Mark's Place and meet me. I had a plausible excuse. St. Mark's Cinema is one of the last revival houses in the city, but it's no place to go alone unless you're Arnold Schwarzenegger.

"I've got to give some stuff to somebody, but he should be there about nine-fifteen. Then we can go and get some Chinese and probably hit the ten o'clock show, okay?"

She said the playbill was *The Women* and *Idiot's Delight*. Gable tap dances. With any luck, I'd be on my way to the hospital instead, with an assault charge against Michael Ruslan in my pocket.

The more I thought about it, the worse I felt about lying-by-omission to Glitter. I could tell myself that the end justified the means, but it never does. Neither does the means justify the end.

Ethics. Promises. The seduction of vendetta.

Goddess, let me get through Saturday night alive and I'll reform. Promise.

Saturday. The sun was still high when I started my preparations for meeting Ruslan—not that you could see it. The sky was an overcast pewter and the air was hazy. I pulled down my shade, lit my candles, and made every other preparation to get ready for tonight.

I had settled the temporal side of the matter;

if Ruslan was obliging enough to break the law in a provable fashion, I would have him prosecuted for it.

That left the spiritual. And what I owed Miriam. Justice.

To call upon the gods for justice in a proper framework of magical ethics, justice alone must be the goal. Not "I win"/"You lose." How can you be sure who will win, if anybody? Maybe *both* of you are wrong. To ask for justice with magic you must care that there is an outcome without caring what it is—the sublime disinterest of the jurist.

That was what I wanted. I would bring Ruslan face-to-face with moral superiority—not mine, because I might not be—and there would be judgment, in which I would take no part.

Magical judgment for magical crimes. Everything else had been leading up to this. And tonight, when what I had set in motion stopped, it would be over for all time.

I watched the candles burn before the Goddess of the Games, and tried to empty myself of hopes for the outcome.

13

There are some odd anomalous nights when the weather goes completely mad. I can never remember whether it's cold air/warm ground or warm air/cold ground that makes fog, but sometimes—even in polluted, overindustrial cities—the conditions are still right.

It wasn't a very heavy fog, but it turned the street lamps into soft balls of golden light and made the geography of the next street over just a little uncertain. There was the lightest of warm misty rains falling; enough to make the air glitter. If the need arose, I could wrap the air around me like a cape. Or walk on it.

And if I fell, that was because there was need for that too, in the glittering patternless design that stretched farther and farther the longer I looked. I was part of that design; I could see the steps that had been laid out for me before I was born, and dance their pattern willfully and foreknowing.

And that I never suspected Ruslan was smart enough to anticipate me, that was foreordained, too.

Below Eighth Street the aseptic grid of Upper Manhattan gives way to a tangle of streets that intersect in any way they please. The *place* in St. Mark's Place where I was meeting Glitter—and Ruslan—was a mostly triangular traffic island built nearly flush with the surrounding asphalt and put there in the hope of unknotting the chaos of five intersecting streets. It contained a lamppost and a god-awful piece of cubist modern sculpture, but was in plain sight of stores, pedestrians, and suicidal motorists driving *en pointe* in the lemming ballet. The fog made things especially chancy.

I achieved the little plaza. Barely. I checked my watch.

I'd told Glitter nine-fifteen. I'd told Ruslan nine-thirty. But it was nine o'clock when I got to St. Mark's Square, and Ruslan was waiting for me.

He stepped out from behind the sculpture, and at first I didn't recognize him. He was wearing a trench coat; he looked like a rumpled, pudgy Bogart, but he wasn't funny.

"Give it to me," he said. No, not funny at all.

I stared at him. I had brought the presence of the Goddess with me; I felt Her as an infinite peace. Even so, I'd been expecting something more confrontational, with rhetoric.

"The book," Ruslan said. He didn't look like someone carrying an *athame*, either. I *knew* he

didn't have it, but I said my lines like I was supposed to.

"We trade."

He pulled something out of his pocket, but it
wasn't Miriam's *athame*. It was a gun.

I stared at it stupidly. *Cold iron breaks all
magic*, I thought, just as if this were a fairy tale
and the gun wasn't real. Traffic whipped by
scant feet away. It might have been on the dark
side of the moon for all the useful help it was.

"Give it to me," Ruslan said. He smiled, and
for an instant we were both in on the joke. Both
of us knew what was to come. Neither of us was
fooled. We had consented to this mystery play a
long, long time ago.

I pulled a red silk bag out of my jacket. I was
wearing the same one I'd worn the night I posted
the flyers, but I was only carrying one thing now.
I turned the bag upside down and shook the
contents out on the ground.

It was the front cover of the missal; I'd
burned the rest of it that afternoon. The wood
was soft; when push came to crunch I'd been
able to split it into nine pieces with my *boline*
and tie each piece up with hand-dyed red wool
yarn and twigs of American mountain ash.

"Rowan tree and red thread." Proof against
all sorcery. I'd knotted feathers into the cords,
and blue glass beads, and a little silver pentacle—binding, purifying, breaking the power of
the Khazar coven over Miriam forever. There was
nothing they could do to her—or her spirit—
now.

Ruslan giggled, and even in my self-induced

trance state I thought it was a bizarre reaction. He waved the gun as if he didn't care who saw it. The fog made haloes around everything.

He looked at me with a weird crinkled little smile on his face. He was sweating; the light reflected off each moving drop as it slid down his cheeks.

Then he looked into my eyes for the first time. I felt a chill shock of kinship even as I realized how far gone he was.

Gone. "A journey to that far country from which no man returns." Meaningless tag-ends of poetry beat through me, and the passage of the cars on the street seemed to take on an intentional rhythm.

Ruslan's smile died like a burnt-out lightbulb. He brought the gun down and settled himself into the brace familiar from a hundred TV shows. I realized that he was going to shoot me now, and that the act wouldn't touch him at all.

The Goddess folded Her wings around me and I stood waiting for some cue to move. There was a letter addressed to the police—it was on my desk at work along with the rest of the Khazar material. Maybe this was the way justice would be served.

Then Ruslan broke stance and stepped backward off the curb—getting ready to run; getting a better angle. I don't know.

There was an impact, soft and heavy at once, like dropping a stone onto a lawn. The gun in his hand vanished like a magician's trick, leaving me blinking after it.

That was when I saw the car. It swerved

wildly out, and then speeded up. I never saw what color it was. I don't know if the driver was even quite sure he'd hit somebody.

Ruslan tottered on his feet for a minute, face thrown back into the mist. Long enough for me to believe he was fine and we'd go on to Act Two. Then he fell and rolled into the gutter at my feet, just like in the movies.

The presence of the Goddess—or just ritually induced euphoria—was gone. Shock made me cold. I knew—good Samaritan, good citizen— that having witnessed a hit-and-run accident, my duty was to summon the authorities.

Ruslan was moving, trying to get up. I knelt down beside him, but I couldn't have said a word if there was money in it for me. His eyelids fluttered. His face was sickly pale, and he didn't seem to be able to move his right arm. There was no blood; only a smear of dirt on the trench coat to indicate impact.

He opened and closed his mouth, but I didn't hear anything. I leaned closer, too stunned to be afraid. There was a rank fruity smell on his breath, and I remembered all those little bottles in the refrigerator in Queens. Michael Ruslan was a diabetic, and by the time the ambulance came and took him to Bellevue Emergency and figured that out, it might be too late for insulin to do any good.

I looked around. No one was paying attention. Nobody in New York pays any attention to anybody else. A lot of people sleep in gutters in New York. Ruslan could be just one more.

My mind raced with the chill hyperlexia of

shock. I thought about a gray cat, fur brown with blood. Nails through its eyes and its mouth and stomach filled with broken razor blades.

I thought about Miriam, alone and afraid. Calling me for help, and dying before I could give it. Hoping even at the end that things could turn out right.

I thought about the Goddess's justice. *Her* justice, not mine.

"Emergency? I need an ambulance. A man has been hit by a car at St. Mark's Place. He's hurt and unconscious. He's a diabetic. I think he's in shock."

The operator said something while I was hanging up. Probably asking who I was.

I'm nobody, who are you?

Are you nobody too?

When I got back to the Square at nine-thirty there was no sign of anyone, including Ruslan. So I went home. There was a message on my machine from Glitter, telling me she had some emergency overtime and couldn't make it.

Gable isn't that good a dancer, anyway.

Ruslan died on the way to the hospital. So I heard. There's a death certificate on file in the county courthouse, and the name and address matches. I looked it up.

Did Miriam Seabrook die of black magic or just liver failure? Does the intent of the person who sincerely wanted her dead not matter just because his tools weren't good enough—if they weren't?

And was I right—never mind effective—to do what I did?

You have your version of the truth and I have mine. I know what killed Miriam. And I know why Ruslan died.

A week later I went up to the apartment in Queens; it was vacant. I told the super a bunch of lies about being from the City Housing Commission; it was enough to make him tell me Ludmilla Ruslan had left suddenly. No warning, no forwarding address.

On the way home I stopped into The Snake. It was fuller than usual. Next Wednesday was August first—Lammas—so last-minute shoppers were stocking up on candles and incense.

I wondered where I'd be celebrating it. Belle hadn't called. I hadn't had the nerve to call her. I wondered if she knew about Ruslan yet.

Julian spoke to me before I'd quite got in the door.

"Bast? I've got your book for you."

I would have ignored him except for the fact that he wasn't up on his throne. He'd come down to floor level to be sure of stopping me. And he was actually making eye contact.

So I followed him back to the cash register, still determined to refuse whatever he came up with, but the package he handed me was too small and lumpy to be a book. It was wrapped in brown paper, and squished with the feel of layered newspaper when I took it. I felt the hard shape of the blade even through the newspaper, but I tore it open to be sure.

Miriam's *athame*. I looked at Julian. He looked past me, meaningfully.

I turned to where he was looking and saw Starfawn. She saw me see her and ran like hell.

Last week I sent a sympathy card to Rachel Seabrook. I didn't put my return address, but I signed the name she'd know. Sometimes I wonder what she did with Miriam's ashes.

THE BEST IN MYSTERY

☐ 51388-6 THE ANONYMOUS CLIENT $4.99
J.P. Hailey Canada $5.99

☐ 51195-6 BREAKFAST AT WIMBLEDON $3.99
Jack M. Bickham Canada $4.99

☐ 51682-6 CATNAP $4.99
Carole Nelson Douglas Canada $5.99

☐ 51702-4 IRENE AT LARGE $4.99
Carole Nelson Douglas Canada $5.99

☐ 51563-3 MARIMBA $4.99
Richard Hoyt Canada $5.99

☐ 52031-9 THE MUMMY CASE $3.99
Elizabeth Peters Canada $4.99

☐ 50642-1 RIDE THE LIGHTNING $3.95
John Lutz Canada $4.95

☐ 50728-2 ROUGH JUSTICE $4.99
Ken Gross Canada $5.99

☐ 51149-2 SILENT WITNESS $3.99
Collin Wilcox Canada $4.99

Buy them at your local bookstore or use this handy coupon:
Clip and mail this page with your order.

Publishers Book and Audio Mailing Service
P.O. Box 120159, Staten Island, NY 10312-0004

Please send me the book(s) I have checked above. I am enclosing $ _____
(Please add $1.50 for the first book, and $.50 for each additional book to cover postage and
handling. Send check or money order only— no CODs.)

Name _____
Address _____
City _____ State / Zip _____
Please allow six weeks for delivery. Prices subject to change without notice.

HIGH-TENSION
THRILLERS FROM TOR

☐ 52222-2 BLOOD OF THE LAMB $5.99
Thomas Monteleone Canada $6.99

☐ 52169-2 THE COUNT OF ELEVEN $4.99
Ramsey Cambell Canada $5.99

☐ 52497-7 CRITICAL MASS $5.99
David Hagberg Canada $6.99

☐ 51786-5 FIENDS $4.95
John Farris Canada $5.95

☐ 51957-4 HUNGER $4.99
William R. Dantz Canada $5.99

☐ 51173-5 NEMESIS MISSION $5.95
Dean Ing Canada $6.95

☐ 58254-3 O'FARRELL'S LAW $3.99
Brian Freemantle Canada $4.99

☐ 50939-0 PIKA DON $4.99
Al Dempsey Canada $5.99

☐ 52016-5 THE SWISS ACCOUNT $5.99
Paul Erdman Canada $6.99

Buy them at your local bookstore or use this handy coupon:
Clip and mail this page with your order.

Publishers Book and Audio Mailing Service
P.O. Box 120159, Staten Island, NY 10312-0004

Please send me the book(s) I have checked above. I am enclosing $ _____
(Please add $1.50 for the first book, and $.50 for each additional book to cover postage and handling. Send check or money order only — no CODs.)

Name _____

Address _____

City _____ State / Zip _____

Please allow six weeks for delivery. Prices subject to change without notice.